# THE SIXTH DAWN

M. F. Alfrey

Books by M. F. Alfrey
Symbionts
The Sixth Dawn

# THE SIXTH DAWN
## and Other Tales of Seodan

## M. F. Alfrey

Copyright © 2021 M. F. Alfrey

All rights reserved

The characters and events portrayed in this book are fictitious. Any similarity to real persons, living or dead, is coincidental and not intended by the author.

No part of this book may be reproduced, or stored in a retrieval system, or transmitted in any form or by any means, electronic, mechanical, photocopying, recording, or otherwise, without express written permission of the publisher.

ISBN: 9798459278071

Cover design by: M. F. Alfrey

# CONTENTS

The Sixth Dawn
Stone Blind
Not seen and Not Heard
All Is in the Orbinall
The Distorting Glass
The Undoing of Uisdean
In Baajar Where Gods Stand Together
Oldest Trick in the Book
Tearblade

# THE SIXTH DAWN

The huge boulder obliterated Grendahl's Apothecary sending a blast wave of glass and cloud of some shimmering powder that smelt like lavender. Yargi tripped as he fled. Skittering at a wild angle led by instinctive feet.

'Too close! Too close!' Yargi muttered to himself as he yanked himself straight. His legs were cumbersome twigs, unfit for fleeing. His head a blown open room through which people, humans mostly, the odd Salfirin, scattered and trampled and pushed and shoved and fought. About the street, they scrambled like insects. Their stone bastion suddenly uprooted, exposing their squirming forms to the unkind world of searing light and noise. Someone cried out. Another boulder came hurtling. Yargi glanced up. *That's no boulder.* Its shape was all wrong. More like a balled-up spider... an iron spider.

Yargi froze, transfixed on that spider-boulder growing bigger and more defined in the smoke and flame-arrow sky.

'Please no,' he whispered to himself. To whatever god or goddess was listening.

'Kid! Crazy kid! Get down!' A stranger yelled.

Yargi twisted to stare, knowing really, he should run.

Crash!

The stranger was suddenly a huge balled up spider-boulder. Yargi jolted. Anguished screams. Mournful cries lamenting lost loved ones. Strangers pleading with strangers for merciful help. The clamour of the besieged city rose to a crescendo and unbearably beyond. The cries, the booms, the dust, the smoke, the flame... the need to hide. A nook. There, just down the slope of rubble, he could—

The iron-spider began to unfurl, one leg at a time. Time. It acquired an odd distended quality as if touched by its master, Isatur the Watcher. In that treacly languid slurring of time, smoke curled ethereal serpentine streamers from fired buildings. One great hazy serpent undulated in the balmy updraft of a burning world and cleared, revealing the dark nook once more.

He bolted in fawnish flight. Gambolling across the river of smashed cobbles, he hurled himself up the rubble of the once harbour ward jail. No real place to go. No real plan. The only semblance of a plan — if it could be called that — was to run.

*Safety.*

Yargi leapt into a dive not caring for the biting stone and toothy remnants of iron bars. He hit hard. Did he scream? If he had, he could not say. The world was a hurtful, piercing, gnawing mouth chewing him up to be swallowed by another darkness. As he slinked through a stalwart half-buried arch, the uproar of men's voices chased him down that dark gullet. Voices. The commanding barks of the city guard. 'Bring it down. Bring it down!' Yargi slid and tumbled and pitched and cartwheeled down an unforgiving rubble slope leaving behind the grinding and ker-chunks of the iron-spider. A city breaker unleashing its wicked mandate.

Like a beaten and wretched dog, he fled the insanity besieging the city of Taz. Up there. A world of livid clamour and grief and magia animated iron-spiders. Tumbling gracelessly in, Yargi halted on his head in dust and mortar. Righting himself, he eased on to an elbow and squinted into the dimness. Not far up, the hole was both an evil eye scowling mean light and a demon's mouth screeching terrors of mekanitek siege engines.

Scanning about this gloomy hole, it was apparent he had discovered an old jailcell. The iron bars of which now lay twisted and dislodged from the stone arch that had swallowed him. Yargi studied his latest hiding place. To his left the bent and bowed remains of the iron barred door, now crushed in half by the weight suddenly bearing down upon its frame, struggled in valiant determination to keep the ceiling up. The stone floor, strewn with mortar and ceiling rubble and straw. The far wall, in the darkness, retreating from the rude light of the waring world above. Then he saw it.

A displaced stone in that far wall. Just proud enough to catch the scant light in a way that underscored it in the gloom. Yargi drove himself closer to the wall, where a wooden bucket emerged in the murky air. The reek of urine was suddenly up his nostrils, on his tongue and against his eyeballs. He pinched his nose, blinked and spat.

Trying his best to ignore the stench, Yargi crouched to the stone wall to examine that protruding block. It had not been dislodged by the calamity that had almost destroyed the cell. No mortar kept it in place. This stone had been carefully removed and replaced with clear intention to conceal.

Still crouched, Yargi clasped the block with his fingertips and wiggled it side to side. He worked it towards him until it slid from his grasp as if suddenly realising its own weight. The block struck and rang a stony protest as it joined its cousins. And then the cell seemed obscenely still and quiet all at once. Yargi gazed into that darkest, most utter black of cavities. A starless winter night where evil things dwelt. Yet another mouth within a mouth. *Just how many times can a person be swallowed into darkness?* he wondered.

Frozen to indecision, Yargi remained captive of the purest dark. Voices in the pitch black. Voices. Ushered from that chaos mouth that might suck him in if he stared too long. Voices within. His childish curiosity spoke, *Reach in. Look and see.* Voices inside him. His mother's cautious clucking warned, *Don't you risk it. Lose your fingers, you will.* Yet, as always, curiosity won out. Yargi scrunched his eyes tight. He gritted his teeth. He plunged his right hand in. Mortar, grit, a stone, something worryingly furry and squishy and... what felt like a book.

Yargi jiggled the object toward him. With a final tug, as if the cavity was loathe to release it, he fell in a heap in with the book on his chest. Yargi held his treasure aloft like a trophy and admired it. His eyes having almost grown accustomed to dim confines of the cell.

A thick leather-bound book. Beaten and well thumbed. Papers had been stuffed in and the whole thing wrapped with a leather thong and tied. The cover glimmered worn goldleaf symbols. Forbidden symbols. Symbols of the six.

Yargi knew little about this six except for what most kids his age nattered about. He knew the most prominent, the diamond, represented the wealth and knowledge of the Salfirin. Reptilian folk, like most all over Seodan, except humans of course. Above that was a lighthouse symbolising the ever stalwart, ever-on-guard nation of Stoum. A nation of hairy amphibians. Behind the lighthouse, rising like a sun, was a gear which stood for the gears of progress and represented humans. Yargi's race. The outcasts of Seodan. The ones all others said did not belong.

To the left were two tusks and a flame. The tusks represented the once proud warriors, the Usk. Formidable in their proportions with great tusks protruding from a stern grim-set mouth. They were also tailless like the Salfirin and the Stoum. The flame signalled the ancient Ever Fire, that burned only for the Diraghoni. The most ancient of the reptilian races of Seodan, rumoured to be shape shifters and even fire and frost and poison breathers. They had tails, so Yargi had been told. He had never seen one but he had heard the rumours. The human word for them was *dragon*. Though, by all accounts, Diraghoni found it an offensive distortion.

To the right was a skull of a bird. That was for the Midites, who were now few in number. Their scattered tribes subsisted entirely in the Scorches. Ominous murmurs and rumour described Midites as feral creatures now. Wholly wild and unpredictably brutish. Again, if the exaggerated mutterings of human city folk could be believed. It seemed to Yargi that humans had a way of turning everything into a monster one way or another. Even themselves. Over the last few sweepscores it had been the Salfirin who were the monsters. Well, one in particular anyhow.

The cell suddenly trembled with the impact of something — perhaps another huge rock crashing into the city. Yargi prayed to the Protector it wasn't one of those iron-spiders. Magiatek city breakers. Great trebuchets would hurl them over the walls and the terrifying animated things would open up in that creepy way of theirs and wreak havoc. The GLAS, the Great Liberation Army of Seodan, had been hurling them over the last few days since the uprising.

Another tremor.

More dust and debris snowed down. Yargi scrutinised the cell. It was crumbling under the weight of the collapsed building above it. The arch through which he had fallen appeared solid. Though, even that was uncertain. He elected to scoot closer to the light, out of the urine-soaked gloom and with his back against a more solid looking wall, he placed the book in his lap, unwound the leather thong and opened it.

It was immediately clear this was some kind of journal. Inside the cover of the leather-bound book were scribbled some notes in the undecipherable language — to him anyway — of Salfirin. The hand was delicate and well-schooled in the arts of writing. Which was not surprising. It was said Salfirin education was superior to all other. Though, Salfirin mostly said that. Salfirin like Emlok.

He was the new monster. It was his GLAS army that was besieging the city of Taz right now. Until the sixth dawn. That was how much time the illustrious leader had given the rebels. On the sixth dawn, he would demonstrate a new horror. A new monster of his great mekanitek army. So the doomsayers claimed. Until then, the GLAS would harry them with boulders and the odd iron-spider.

The city had been Emlok's... once.

At least until the last batch of executions. In fact, one of them had been a Salfirin. Not all of them were insane with power like Emlok it seemed. Some even earned death at his hands.

Shaking the ugly thought, Yargi examined the first page. He stroked it, admiring the slightly rough texture. The crispness. He sniffed it. The ink vital and alive. Before he knew it, he was reading...

*The first page. The first journey. So much alike in their*

*stark promise. So much alike in the apprehension they each invoke. Whether as author or journeyman, we hold our breath in anticipation of what dwells in that emptiness, asking: what will I write or where will I go?*

*What should I write?*

*I should probably begin with my name. In the event that I am lost this journal will at least surface. Books have such a habit. Like some forgotten or unknown treasure waiting to be discovered. Though sincerely I hope this will not be the case. That it will merely serve as a library for the tales and lore I mean to accumulate. Yet facts cannot be ignored. We are entering perilous times. Though, I fear few comprehend precisely how treacherous these times will be.*

*My name is Duyen Fian, which is not so important. I am Salfirin, which is. I am a chronicler and this is not so vital to know, but indeed, is vital to my work and has led me to where I find myself right now. Since I was seven sweepscores old, I have garnered a fascination for the written word. That I am Salfirin will no doubt give rise to hateful prejudice amidst most and, at the least, disdain in others. Not all beings are wicked and corrupt, and this goes for my people also. Moreover, we were once a benevolent people. At least, that is how our history would have it.*

*I write herein, mostly in the common tongue of humanity. I believe it to be the most pervasive way to disseminate that which I discover. The human language has ranged far and wide and has achieved as firm a toehold in our world as much as its originators have. They have also lost as much as they have won. Therein rests equilibrium.*

*As a scholar of the arts and languages, I am proficient in all six major tongues of Seodan and several dialects. And what is my intent? I aspire to nothing more than a rekindling of what was lost of our world due to the Cataclysm centuries ago. To some, it is merely a word. A word for some obscure event that set in motion a change. A metamorphosis across Seodan. Yet, it is a word divorced of the gravity it deserves. Gravity, time has assuaged.*

*So it is to the Scorches I turn my attention and scholarly eye. Those vast swathes of altered lands. Twisted and contorted lands. Lands that whisper and on occasion screech stories of foreboding and awe. Yet, in the Scorches are not simply wild things and creatures transmogrified by magia fallout, but people. Tribes, hamlets, villages and towns... they are out there. Isolated. Tiny pockets of our history. History, I fear, soon to be wiped out.*

*It is in great shame, as a Salfirin, that I flee my homeland of the North, to head on my journey. Malghus Emlok has grown to be a powerful voice for my people. They listen to him. Heed his words. And those abominations he is amassing, those magiatek soldiers, alarm me. I do not see the protection he claims they will bring. I see control. I see fear. I see force. Already Emlok's Adjudicators have commenced seizing literary works he has deemed as inciting either dissidence, injurious fiction or both. He will not be content until absolutely all traces of the Old World and its peoples have vanished.*


A tremor shook the crumbling cell again jerking Yargi from the scrawled text. He held his breath so he could listen. The throbbing of his own blood in his ears seemed set to work against him. The thud-thunk-thud-thunk above grew louder and the light vanished. He imagined spiders. Giant iron ones.

*No. No. Nobody's here. Go away.*

The untimely night lingered a moment and then a sudden, blinding new day skipped a harsh dawn into his eyes. He squinted and turned his hungry focus on the book, trying to regain his reading eyes. Yargi stared at this Salfirin's beautifully inscribed mind. He breathed out and in again and read on.


*This is by far the most bizarre of writings I have discovered. Whilst exploring the Scorches of Rhodethå and the Isle of Stonå. The Stoum, a famously hirsute people, have many legends of the lost Bridge City of Nus. None visit this place now. Most are too afraid. East Rhodethå is a wild land of rugged crag-strewn forest, labyrinthine and tortuous to the wanderer.*

*Finding a guide willing to venture there is a form of torture in itself. Ultimately, I was obliged to assemble all the lore and sketches of scraps of maps and copies of historical tomes and local whispers and hearsay to piece together safe passages from the market city of Anorkas.*

*Upon arriving at the bridge city, several days of hard trek and trips and falls and waking nights later, all my hopes seemed sunk. The wooden drawbridge had long disintegrated. The battlements and abutments were crumbled and overgrown in parts and in others, whipped by a malicious tempestuous sea. What struck me most was an eery whistling song issuing from down below. The source was hidden from sight. Tracing that sound led my gaze to a where a section of the bridge had fallen.*

*Now the poet in me would have some muse, perhaps one of Gastian the Protector's kin, sent forth to draw me safely across. Or perhaps the song was the manifestation of one of the sirens of Imia, risen to lure me into the depths and ultimately to Imia's underworld domain. Either way, I convinced myself this crumbling block was the only way across. Treacherous as it may be, if the stories were true, it would be worth the venture.*

*I meandered my way down a jagged natural stair in the cliff to the great carved block that bridged the mainland and isle. On all fours against the wrenching wind and salt spray, I crawled and sprawled my way across. It was now I heard another sound. A sound I had read about and understood should terrify me. It clamoured about me, this screeching, rasping and flapping. The mere weight of it was enough. I stared ahead freezing my route in my mind and slipped my headscarf about my eyes. Closing them beneath, as the writings and warnings advised, I prayed to Gastian my memory would serve well enough.*

*I clambered like a sprawling lizard part of the way and, eventually, with unfounded confidence and not a small part of Salfirin ego I might add, boldly went on. I slipped and fell. I may have cried out. If that was the case, the sea wind swallowed my foolishness. Gastian, indeed, was with me.*

*I landed in a solid heap rather than the ocean. I felt my way along a wall to where the voice of the sea grew faint until I could go no further. I followed that unnerving song and ignored the screeches and flapping of beasts about me. When all that was left was that whistling song, I removed my blindfold and saw I had come to the barnacle encrusted foundations of the city.*

*Above, beyond a gap I would leap, lay the beginning of a mossy stair which led upward to the city proper. It was a slick-in-places windswept climb towards the city ingress. It was here whilst regathering my nerves I came across lichen growing in the most curious pattern trailing up the stair. At first, I thought I had gone mad with solitude. Words! Letters grown in florets of minuscule life. Faded stag's horn blue, bleached out florets of green, punctuated with fruticose growths and wagging beards of old men. The lichen spread a poem, or perhaps a lament of sorts. So, I began to read. Climbing the zig-zagging stair upward with each new verse, quill in hand, I began to record the voice of the city.*

# STONE BLIND

Like I, she cannot see — girl
singing lamentations. Rebounding
my many arches, stirring my foundations.
Trembling my piers, vibrating balustrades,
ringing keystones. Winged creatures come

listen. Luring, her sonorous rhymes,
bring to roost lowly sea-moistened
weed-hemmed arches. Foundations,
granite hewn, so too my breakwaters
and quays. Shielding grand stone

buttresses against the mighty sea —
now softened. Waves channel between
limestone cliffs; isles I bridge. The

sightless girl lures in winged ones as well
as ships in whistling songs. Sailors shun;

they cry witch! Enchantress! Neither is
she. Simply a girl, born blind like me.
She cannot see the screeching beasts
sailors dare not glance nor anger,
least they risk a petrifying

stare. The winged ones relish the dark;
adore the spray. They delight the way their
shrillness echoes broad arches. Stout folk
built me from quarried ageless mountains.
Deep they delved way back. My parapets, my

towers, the curtain walls about the bailey
defending the ruler's keep. From gatehouse
to barbican, along battlements all. From
machicolations with their murder holes,
to gravest, dingy dungeons. Hardy,

unmoving granite am I. Many speak
and shout of my fame. I hear all. If only
walls could talk; my voice would thunder.
Like waves crashing against my broad
piers; deep, too deep, I hear whispers.

Too deep delving in mountains where my
parent rock lies; Old Home. Home of one —
of root and peak. Living stone cracked and
split and carved and hewn. In many parts,
brought separately to coast. Bridge upon

bridge upon bridge upon bridge.
Arches and loop-holes through which
the wind howls, whistles and sometimes
whispers. My only voice in tune with her —
the sightless girl. Deep! I hear peasants'

grumbles. Deep! Nobles and knights alike.

Soft feet fled, steel clad boots advancing.
Scraping and scratching. Familiar, tremendous.
I recall tremors of creatures. Beasts once
imprisoned. From beneath the mountains

that bore me, they came. From
the isle I am split — the drawbridge
is lifted. Yet it mattered not; the pit
between cliff and gatehouse. The beasts
are in, the climbers and their claws and

their calls. Reverberating, my walls sing
of steel, gouges, scrapes and scratches.
Talon and blade, I fear neither; I do not
bleed as they so do. Soon, drenched
red with both builder and beast, my

defences overrun. They hang from
turret and merlon, perch in crenels
between. I hear her then, the sightless

girl, she sings her pets to skitter and
scratch and squawk, taking to the wing.

Stone makers these winged ones. With central
eyes open. They soared and swooped.
The mountain beasts stiffened,
grasping ashlar stone, grown cold, flesh
now granite, grimaces fixed longing for

breath. The winged ones descended,
returning to roost. The sightless girl
now in a hush. I hear no feet, no
whispers of folk in bailey or keep.
Though I feel them. All remain; beast,

peasant, noble, knight. At one with walls
battlements and turrets. They stand now stone,
gargoyles and grotesques. Forever against sea
and salt-wind. Blind as the girl who alone
still sings. In buttress nook to her

ones winged. She whistles eternal

to generations of stone. Each and

the other moss and lichen grown.

\* \* \*

*As I ascended, translating the lichen into a more conventional and legible hand, I noticed the whistling song which had originally drawn me had grown closer. Or rather I had grown closer to it. Atop the stair, beneath that final mossy stanza, lay at rest the huddled bones of what I could only guess were the remains of the girl of whom the city walls spoke. She was singing still, to this very day, the wind whistling through her bones.*

'Walls that write?' Yargi lay the book in his lap and imagined such a thing. Truly? Such things exist? He had never ventured out of Taz. Least, not that far. The Ringwood perhaps, for mushrooms and berries. Though not since the GLAS arrived. Before the rebellion, they had imposed a curfew and no one was permitted beyond the gates without the proper mark on their papers. Papers folk did just fine without before. Papers too expensive to acquire for most.

The subterranean cell had grown quiet and Yargi wondered if the siege was over for a few foolish seconds. *I should look. See if I can find a safer place to hide.* But the journal shifted in his lap and the next page, perhaps caught by a breeze coming in through the arch above, turned, as if inviting him to remain.

'Okay,' he told the ink crowded pages, 'one more...'

*What follows is a tale I recorded on my extensive travels of the Draiochtarian Coast. Emlok's forces are yet to harry the fishing villages surviving out here in the Scorches. None are great enough to pose a strategic advantage I imagine. The lack of Emlok's Enforcers means the locals are a little more amenable to conversation and imparting tales and lore with outlanders without fear of reprisal. Speaking to a few, I can see in their eyes the disbelief of how one could be imprisoned for merely sharing old tales. I pray they never experience the miserable truth first-hand.*

*For this tale, I am certain it is fact rather than legend or myth. When I arrived in the modest agricultural village of Ham, it was clear something was peculiar. Yet I found it a trial to put a word or phrase to it at the time. They have only one tavern there. The Old Yolk. The least hospitable of places to be honest. Yet not through animosity towards strangers, even for a Salfirin such as myself. I received a few gasps and the occasional inquisitive glance when I removed my hood upon entering, though nothing ever came of it. The human locals merely returned to nursing their ale and idle muttering.*

*I made for the bar and keep who stood discussing wheat yields with a farmer and all the terrible weather lately. It required a clearing of my throat and an uneasy greeting before he acknowledged me. I asked him of the village, of which he said little, so I elected to bear my warm ale to a lone table in the corner under the watchful gaze of an elderly lady with the overbite of a deep-sea fish and two mutton-chopped men with broad forearms and lines in their faces like thirsty earth.*

*I sat a while before the place started to fill and liven up in that lacklustre way I was becoming accustomed to. It was about then the barmaid, Elva, arrived. She caught my eye since she seemed the sole person in the*

*Old Yolk that had any vibrance about her. Her skin was rosy with the vigour of life. Her eyes keen as a blade cutting through the meaning of existence itself. It was she who struck up conversation with me.*

*Ham was not the kind of place people visited, she said. I informed her briefly of my pursuits and journey so far. She was particularly attentive to the war and what was out in the Scorches. So we made a deal. I would expound all I knew if she disclosed a local story to me. What I thought would be an evening occurrence transformed into several days of us meeting together. I took everything down. What she imparted to me brought a lump in my throat and the habit of suspecting everyone in the village except her. It was during the coach journey to Ensum beyond Sand Back Bay, that I immortalised her story in these pages.*

# NOT SEEN AND NOT HEARD

She plumped her bottom lip. Sulking eyes moistened with petulant almost-tears. 'I don't want to,' Elva insisted. She stamped a foot and bunched her fists so hard she imagined her skin creaking and cracking.

'I won't have this behaviour,' said Mother. 'I won't. Elva dear, you simply must do as you are told.' Mother turned to the hearth, proving she could not care less.

'The day has run away with me. He'll be expecting his supper and with the evening coming in as it is, I simply can't leave. What with your little sister so sick...'

'But he's *peculiar*,' said Elva. Her cheeks blossomed warmth, but not from the hearth. She stuttered for more to say, yet nothing would come so she gritted her teeth instead.

Shea wailed and Mother left the hearth, stepping across their modest dwelling to her baby sister's meagre crib. She reached down cooing and tutting, scooping Shea up in her arms.

Elva scowled, focusing her rage to a sharp point, stabbing at her pale little sister with it. 'She's always sick,' she said.

She made no effort to bother veiling the jealousy and bitterness she felt towards Shea anymore. Elva had done so once, hoping things would change — that she would be noticed again. Things had gotten worse, not better. Her folks only seemed to notice her when she misbehaved. Just like now.

Perhaps hate would seem too harsh an emotion to be directed at a babe. Yet, ever since Shea had come along, Elva failed to attract her mother's attention and whenever she attempted to help, she was told to stop fussing. The switch from Elva to this little sickly grey thing Mother and Father called *daughter*, this thing they insisted she called sister, had been swift. The discovery on their doorstep. The decision to keep her. The endless cooing. The endless wailing.

Elva's parents had argued of course. Mother had won — she always won. She had maintained that no decent folk would ever see such a delicate babe out in the cold, especially not with wild midites and rabid onskogs skulking the fringes of

Ringwood. The mining of the Ulvern Mountains had disturbed such creatures, pushing them from feasting on wild animals to stalking the village of Ham.

'To be without the warmth and love a good family could shower upon a babe,' Mother had said, 'to be a morsel for such wretched creatures as them. Terrible, terrible thing to do.'

Elva had never wanted a little sister.

What she wanted, though, seemed not to matter. Her sulks and refusals were her protests. Now, however, was one of those instants where Shea was innocent of blame. Elva protested with all the spark and fire she could manage because the idea of taking Old Sneft his supper gnawed at all her childish insecurities and flushed nightmares out from their hiding places.

Mother walked over to the hearth bouncing baby Shea in one arm. Despite Mother's straining efforts to please and comfort her, baby Shea persisted in her screams. She wanted her supper too. Elva knew the pitch all too well.

It was different to other times. When she was hungry, Shea screamed so hard it made *Elva's* throat sore. How red raw it must be. How it must pain her. However, the pity stopped short. For the screams persisted for far too long. Even wild vuvek would howl in sympathy for Shea. There was something feral about that child. The vuvek knew it. Elva knew it. Yet Mother and Father seemed ignorant of the fosterling's untamed nature.

With her free hand, Mother scooped up the fresh bread that had been cooling on the table by the hearth and tucked it into bed in the wicker basket she always carried Old Sneft's supper in. She came towards Elva with lips spread thin and a do-as-you're-told frown. She thrust the basket out.

Sniffing and turning away, Elva stuck her lip out further, folded her arms and stamped again. 'No!' She heard Mother set the basket on the slate floor and step back to the hearth, jostling screeching baby Shea up and down.

'There it shall remain until you take it. I have no time for your tantrums. Father will be home and wanting to be fed.'

Shea belted another intense screech and Elva felt her skin prickle and her insides twist. It was a sound she had grown to loathe. So frequent it was, she even heard it in her dreams. Baby Shea had ruined everything.

Mother tutted. 'Yes, yes. You'll eat too. My you are so grumpy around this time, aren't you?' she said to little Shea, kissing her forehead as though she were a delicate egg. 'My! You are stone cold still — won't you ever warm up?' She turned to Elva, glared at the basket, then Elva again.

Unfolding her arms with a huff in the most dramatic way she could muster, Elva swooped to whisk up the basket not caring for the contents. She spoke no words as she marched peevish steps out of their cramped cottage into the frigid winter eve and set off down the dirt track. The only thoroughfare in the forgettable coastal village of Ham.

It was a dreary old place in summer, let alone the winter. The Great Anokas Sea was always a silver-grey blanket which appeared seamlessly sewn to the storm-plagued horizon. When she was old enough, Elva promised herself she would sneak on a ship and leave for the Diraghoni Isles.

There, the Diraghoni still roamed free. The last of a great reptilian people. Once their culture had dominated the lake lands of Salosnareth and the mountainous region of Dafadares. Regal masters of magia. So exciting, unlike Ham. Yes, she would run away, see the world. Most likely her folks would not even miss her.

Somewhere in the freezing mists, a vuvek howled. Elva clutched the basket tight to her chest, the smell of freshly baked bread her only comfort. The vuvek was distant, however, and with each plaintive howl seemed a good distance further from Ham.

Naturally, as Elva relaxed, her bothersome mind turned to Old Sneft. She swung his supper in the crook of her arm plodding reluctantly down the rutted track. Grooves already frozen by the stiff sea breeze. Like all reclusive folk, Sneft unnerved the village children. Despite being the eldest, Elva felt no different.

Not that she had seen much of him. He had about him a peculiar appearance. Shrivelled and shrunken by the years. Skin loose, pallid and grey. Face forever veiled beneath the tatty, threadbare hood he always wore. The grownups in the village joked he was the goddess Conus, the Bringer of Death, in mortal form.

Surely, Sneft wasn't, was he? Elva's childish mind fought the other, more adult one. The one that seemed more dominant nowadays. The one that fired her temper and goaded her protests.

Sneft rarely spoke. When he uttered anything, it was not language but grunts and beastly sounds that could almost be mistaken for words. Nowadays, Sneft rarely ever left his rundown cottage on the edge of the village. Only at such times when his supper was forgotten. He would visit Elva's cottage and skulk there waiting for Mother to feed him. Darkness seemed to find Old Sneft. Forever in shadow he was. Even where shadows should not linger. Not naturally, anyhow.

Such visits were rare now and Elva thanked Salaria for such fortunate infrequency. Mother became — at those moments — ham-fisted, inept and fumbling. It seemed that everything that could possibly go wrong, would. Mother claimed nothing but nerves on her part; that being watched whilst working always put her off.

'Where are you going?' came a high-pitched squeal from behind. Elva knew the voice well, it was Casee, the younger boy from the cottage down from hers. She turned her head to greet him, ensuring her face displayed her discontent and said in an offended voice, 'Old Sneft's.'

Muddy faced and scruffy haired as usual, Casee wrinkled his nose and stuck out his tongue at the sound of the name. 'Why are you going there?'

Elva patted the basket dangling at the crook of her arm. She stood a good two heads taller than Casee and she found herself looking down at him. 'Supper time, and mother's busy with the brat.'

Casee shrugged and fell in step alongside her. 'Yeah... I heard her yammering. The vuvek too. You hear them as well, I s'pose?'

Elva nodded but remained mute.

'I'll walk with you if you like,' said Casee in a sympathetic manner which most children in Ham understood. Everyone was fearful of Old Sneft, including some of the grownups. 'He's a morlig you know,' said Casee, picking his nose and looking at the contents as if considering whether it was edible or not.

Elva squirmed. 'Eur, that's gross Casee.'

'I know. Morligs are bad luck when they're not fed.' He wiped his finger on his grubby tunic, adding another streak.

Elva rolled her eyes, she meant him not morligs. It would be pointless explaining, Casee wasn't the sharpest chisel in the chest. 'You'll believe anything,' she said. 'Anyway, that's not possible.'

'Why ain't it?' said Casee, stuffing his hands in the pockets of his rough spun trews. He always did that when he felt someone was about to oust him as a fool. 'He's short like one. Who's ever heard of a hundred-year-old man what's no taller than a child?'

'My mother says folk shrink when they get old,' said Elva in an authoritarian adult voice. She paused to adjust her dress so it looked more proper, then carried on walking.

'Rubbish!' snorted Casee. 'Anyway, he don't never talk or ought and bad stuff happens when he's hungry.'

'My mother says he just makes folk nervous and that's why things go wrong when he's around.' She looked ahead, Old Sneft's place materialised like some dark crumbling ancient castle in the mist.

Invisible or floating at its rocky roots, yet threatening and wicked like some monstrous looming giant.

'My mother says, my mother says...' said Casee in his most irksome imitation of Elva. 'Is that all you can say? He's a morlig, I tell you. Me dad says so. So do most folk in the Old Yolk. I've heard them talking. Bad luck when they're not fed, good luck when they're kept happy...'

'That's just ale-talk, stupid. My mother — people say, most men don't know truth from fantasy when they've had a few.' It was true. She had witnessed her father returning from that tavern many times not making any kind of sense but truly believing he did.

They both paused.

They had finally come to Old Sneft's cottage. Casee was struck dumb in an instant, gaze fixed on the grey stone dwelling. The mossy thatch had rotted into clumps of shaggy haired severed heads. A stalk's nest sat abandoned in a chimney. The stalk long flown or maybe even eaten by the old man himself.

Elva drew in a deep breath and strode toward the crooked hardwood door on the exhale. She looked back at Casee before she knocked and jerked her head for him to join her. He shook his vehemently. Rolling her eyes again, as she often did when Casee was around, Elva rapped on the wooden door.

The sound was dull and Elva doubted Old Sneft had even heard her soft knuckles glance that splintered door. Her clenched fist hovered in place for a moment — so painfully white and soft against the coarse darkness of that door. Elva allowed three swift breaths until she finally gave up the idea of knocking again.

Silence pressed heavy on Elva's shoulders as she began to step down. The doorstep suddenly felt the most exposed sea cliff in the world. A dead world where withered things struggled to grow and pitiful insects writhed. Not a thing grew in Old Sneft's garden; not even green-needled winter trees. The cottage walls were crumbling and the window frames spongey and bowed with rot.

Her mother's voice picked up in her head and with it the weight of the trouble she would be in if she returned with a full basket. Too terrified to eat the contents herself and lie, Elva resigned to face that dark door and knock a little louder. She raised her free hand and clenched the basket tightly in the other.

The latch dropped so loudly Elva leapt down a whole step and nearly fell. Casee's chuckles brought a fierce sneer from her only for her attention to be wrenched back to the door as it scraped open on hinges shrieking for a good oiling.

'Mus?' came a grunt Elva took for greeting.

She held up the basket in silence; words swollen in her throat. The door opened slightly further and a macabre inquisitiveness consumed Elva, forcing her gaze into the darkness. The door receded a little in response to her inquisitive eyes and she felt embarrassed at her own prying. Her mother had always told her not to be nosey and not to stare because it 'don't sit well with most folk.' Children — especially — should be seen and not heard.

Elva hurriedly averted her gaze, still holding the basket out. A creak of wicker and she felt the hand grasping the handle brush hers. It was a frigid stone touch, yet rough, like lichen smothered limestone. Elva stifled a yelp and thought she should say something but all words and sounds dammed up against a wall of clenched teeth. She felt suffocated as though she were far beneath the surface of some frigid murky lake, drowning.

'Mank yuh,' said Sneft and the door closed with an abrupt grating slam.

Dashing back from the cottage to Casee, Elva felt nothing of the stony ground beneath her feet and thought of nothing but the old man's rasping touch. Casee laughed stupidly, tears streaming down his mucky cheeks leaving pink tracks.

'You should've seen yerself!' he guffawed as they walked back towards Elva's home. 'Who'll believe anything now, eh?'

She scowled at him, but said nothing. All Elva could do was stroke away the lingering iciness in her right hand where Old Sneft had brushed her skin. The fleeting glimpse of him lingered in her mind all the way back. It was if he had taken up residence in her head, refusing to leave.

She hardly noticed Casee say goodbye, still chuckling to himself as he went home. She barely touched her stew when sat at the table with her folks whilst baby Shea finally slept in her crib. She only just acknowledged Father reprimanding her earlier fuss. She scarcely even noticed his usual tired line about being seen and not heard.

So preoccupied was Elva, that she helped Mother tidy away after supper without protest. As mother set the kettle for their usual evening drink of barley tea, she went about a few tasks ready for the next day and her mind naturally turned to preparing Old Sneft's basket.

'Oh,' said Mother, pressing a hand to her mouth in thought. 'Where's the basket, Elva?'

'Basket?' said Elva, who was now considering changing out of her dress and into her bedclothes, hoping the amnesia of sleep would make her feel better.

'Mr. Sneft always puts out the basket shortly after he's taken his food.'

Holding her breath, Elva shifted from foot to foot anticipating what would come next. Her chest felt tight and she wished there was some place in the cottage she could sculk like a mouse hiding from a prowling farm cat. Elva looked outside at the dwindling light hoping Mother would not ask her to retrieve the basket.

'He didn't give it back,' Elva blurted. 'He slammed the door — he was very rude.' Elva hoped the excuse would work in her favour. Mother rested her hands on her hips and flashed Elva *that* look. Elva knew she had already pushed her luck too much today.

'Well, you didn't wait long enough. He's an old man Elva... he takes his time, and yes, he can be a little curt. Yet I've never taken him as rude. He's a well-respected man and has been so for quite some time.' Mother looked out at the world. 'There's still a little light left in the day. Hurry and fetch it, would you?'

Elva wanted to cry so badly, but knew it would do no good. With pleading eyes, she looked to Father who was sat in the corner with his feet up smoking his pipe.

'Don't look at me,' he said between puffs and went back to gazing at the crackling pine logs.

Mother raised an eyebrow and Elva gave up and left for Old Sneft's again.

The walk back to Sneft's seemed longer somehow. Prolonged and elongated by dread and ruthless imaginings which plagued Elva worse than daemons. Elva's recollections of Sneft were now a melancholy collage of the warped memories of a child and stories from the likes of Casee and ale-headed rumour.

She tripped, but caught herself halfway in the fall, hand and one knee down in the now frozen dirt. When she rose, it was as if the light had suddenly been stolen in those fleeting moments and all that remained was the star-speckled night.

A bright winter moon, impossibly huge, illuminated the dirt road which unfurled in a silver shimmer. An icy tongue leading her down the throat of the night. Every footfall came sluggishly and lurid as if she were a titanic Berganor, the fabled mountain giants — the Juns of legend.

She surely felt no mightier than a worm. Yes, a worm. Exposed to the gnawing frost above its warm soil world. Alone. Headed towards the morlig's lair.

Silly.

Silly Casee. Elva's mind trundled over and over.

How could the old man be a morlig? He had been known in the village for almost a century. Yes, he was very old but everyone attributed that to wealth and prosperity. Mother called him Lucky Old Sneft from time to time and Elva had heard the very same from others too. Lucky to live so long, they would say. Just gone a bit reclusive in his years, that was all.

Old Sneft's decaying cottage was bearing over her before Elva knew it. How has a lucky person settled to live in a village like Ham and in such a tumble-down barn as this? It made not much sense to her, but then Elva assumed that she lacked adult understanding because, as Father said, she was a child and children knew very little.

Elva's heart sank to her toes as she scanned the doorstep wishing the empty basket to be there — waiting. Instead, the slate step stared back vacant and mocking. She considered turning around, even started to move away, but again worrying what Mother might say, she swallowed hard and climbed the steps.

Had there been so many? And had they been so steep before? Elva asked herself over and over as she made her way up. Had she been too preoccupied with her task that the steps had simply gone unnoticed? Or had they grown protruding from the soil in her absence? In fact, as she huffed upward, the cottage seemed to shift and morph in the moonlight as though it breathed. Some great cottage-beast now awoken by the absence of sunlight and a bewitching moon.

Finally, Elva reached the topmost step. Closing her eyes, she knocked.

She waited.

An owl screeched a shiver through her body in the moonlight. In the distance a vuvek hailed a giant frosted moon and conjured images of the giant wolf-like monsters prowling in the night. She opened her eyes; the door remained closed. Every part of Elva's being desired to leave, but guilt and fear of Mother's reprimands forced her knuckles to rap once again.

Silence echoed back and nothing more.

Pressing gently on the door, Elva found it give inwards slightly. Unlocked? Perhaps intentionally. She wondered if the basket were just inside the door. She could grab it and be gone in a few soft steps. Elva eased the door a little more, ensuring no creak or squeak escaped the antiquated hinges.

It was icy inside. The air stale with the odd tinge of something unlike anything Elva had ever known. No lingering softness of baked bread, no smoky residue of a fire hanging in the air, no pipe smoke nor sour remanence of ale. It smelt like a stable, not a home. Clamping nostrils between thumb and finger, Elva narrowed her eyes in search of the basket in the grainy darkness.

In a stoop, Elva searched the floor just inside the door with her free hand; grit and dirt, but nothing else. Then she heard it. Like some slumbering boar in the darkness — the rolling snores of a deep sleeper. If he was asleep, then how would she retrieve the basket? What would Mother say? Elva stepped into the icy fetid air hoping, for once, she would not be seen nor heard.

As her eyes adjusted, the interior of the cottage faded into ambiguous soft edges. Unknown shapes grew into actual recognisable objects Elva managed to guess by logic of what a person would generally find in a cottage.

A great leering skeleton in ragged clothes shrank into the shape of a crowded coat stand. The sweeping form of a slumbering reptilian Onrake became the chairs and table beneath a dusty sheet. Two black cats with gleaming eyes became a pair of boots with polished silver buckles. The hearth was dead and black, glinting dimly in the moonlight that struck in through the doorway in a supernatural blade. Her own shadow cast up against the grill to distort and quiver like grinding black teeth.

Once all had appeared to her as it was, the snoring seemed loud again and clearly placed in a dark corner of the cottage to her right. Elva froze, hoping her breath would be as quiet as a leaf in a breeze. To her, it sounded as violent as a storm. Her breath and the snoring, was all she could hear.

Narrowing her eyes to slits so severe they were almost closed, that corner became so clear. The slumbering bulk of Old Sneft, like a barrow in the moonlight, rising and falling gently and there, beside his bed was the basket. Elva sighed and tiptoed over through the fingers of moonlight creeping in through unseen holes.

In a matter of heart-fluttering seconds, she found herself right beside Old Sneft who was hidden beneath a pile of musty blankets. Elva's feet were inches away from the basket. She stooped slowly, cringing as her dress suddenly seemed the roughest, scratchiest thing in the world. Her little pale fingers, so clear and luminous in the darkness they seemed to glow, wrapped around the handle. She lifted it so gently, so carefully, that the whole action seemed to take an eon.

Casting her glance to the door, light sifting in through the gap, she followed that clear-cutting slice of light to the back of the cottage. Could see clearly what she had not been able to distinguish before. Now, from this improved angle, she could see Old Sneft sat in a time-addled armchair, sunken pits of eyes staring into nothingness.

She sucked in her breath and bit her lip so hard it bled. She clutched the basket close to her in both hands as though it were a great wooden shield. The snoring continued behind her, beyond her ability to understand how the old man could be in two places at once. Then, as terrible as it was, her eyesight improved even more, soaking up as much silver light as it could, she saw clearly that it was indeed Old Sneft in that chair. Not the pallid grey fellow she had glimpsed earlier, but the gaunt yellowed remains of the man, his decayed smile jeering her.

The snoring behind her became a choking, throttled spluttering urging Elva's feet, first in a backwards shuffle, then a dash for the door. She dared not to look back. The rustle of sheets — a brutish sniffing. Her heart bounded and eyes grew wide with imaginings of the horrifying creature behind her. The creature that had been impersonating Old Sneft. Casee, the drunken men of the Old Yolk... had been right in their gossiping. It was a morlig that dwelt here. A morlig!

She skittered all the way to the door. Creeping coldness pursuing her. Hurrying dragging steps. Something coming — raspy fingertips raked her hair.

Elva shrieked.

She tugged her hair free of the morlig's grasp.

Fell out into the moonlit night. She ran. Down the steps, along the path, up the dirt track, over rut and rock. A backward glance and she stifled another shriek. The thing was chasing her. Hobbling in a lurching motion just shy of natural as if incapable of fluid and graceful movement.

It hissed. A foul, livid escape of air. A scream lingering on the scratchy pull of its breath. A mucus bubbling gargle. The dreadful noises hurried Elva's feet. The dread hauling her towards the village — towards home. She glanced back again. The figure was suddenly motionless. It shrieked furiously into the night as if it were several beasts, not one. Clasping at its chest with one hand, the other clawing the air where Elva had been. It collapsed to its knees, remained stiffly upright as it stubbornly tried to breathe its last and failed. The morlig tumbled forward like a tree slow to realise it had been felled. There its body clenched and curled, face down in the dirt.

Elva stopped, lingering against all her instinct. She crept to the motionless lump in the road. Had it died? Had the sudden excitement been too much for it? Closer, closer and closer she came until she stood over it. The morlig, for it could have been nothing other than that, was dead. Murdered by exertion and old age. The grey creature lay spread on the ground in Old Sneft's clothes, as lifeless as the real Mr. Sneft back at the cottage.

Bravery taking hold, Elva knelt to examine what looked like a man at a glance, in poor light, but out in the revealing moonlight was most certainly something too twisted and grotesque to be human. Yet it was indeed ancient, evidenced by the thin spinney of white hair on its balding pate. Hands, grey and clawed, feet shoeless and long-toed with curling yellow nails like tree roots.

Elva shivered.

She gasped as the morlig receded in on itself. It shrank away until only clothes lay on the dirt track. That was enough for Elva. She dashed back home as quickly as she could.

Nothing was the same after that. People treated her gently, being the child that had discovered the old man's corpse. Such a sad affair that he had died so suddenly yet death had left him in such an advanced state of decay. Folk blamed wood spirits for the condition of his corpse. Elva told her mother about the morlig so many times the story began to sound too like a child's fable, even to her own ears.

Elva even began to believe the adults' claim that it was merely the fantastic imaginings of a child. That wounded the deepest. Mother not hearing her. She told Casee, he believed. So, did the other children of Ham. But slowly, one by one, over time as Elva grew, the people of Ham became more adept at not seeing and not listening. Casee no longer left the house and when Elva had last visited him, he remained hidden inside mumbling more like and animal than a boy. His mother made excuses for him in one breath and, in the other, remarked on how her luck had recently picked up on the farm after Casee's illness.

Elva never returned to see Casee again. She had seen in through the door, in the back, the pale little creature dressed as her friend. She often wondered if his mother knew, or if she was too overcome with grief to admit her son had been replaced. Or perhaps she was just infatuated with the family's turn of fortune. People of Ham seemed to get luckier and luckier each passing season.

One evening, returning home from the fields with Father after reaping one of the biggest harvests they could ever remember, Elva had sat with her parents and the perpetually sick adopted sister of hers. She observed Shae, swaddled in blankets, Mother complaining of the persisting pallid complexion and stone coldness of Shae's skin to Father who ate and drank taking not that much notice, like most in Ham.

Elva sighed as she ate her supper wondering if the people of Ham were really that foolish or if they were glad with the village's sudden flourishing luck. Wondering if Mother or Father had even noticed they were nursing a morlig. Wondering if she would just become accustomed to it like everyone else. Perhaps... if she stopped seeing and hearing. Perhaps then.

He closed the book with a shudder. *Morligs?* Yargi had heard tales. Children's yarns, though. Myth, right? But here, this Duyen, claims them to be real? He glanced up to the half-buried arch and strained to imagine the world beyond it. Beyond the shattered city. Beyond its ring of woodland. Truly out there — out in the Scorches.

'I need to escape Taz, don't I?' he asked the book. Its gnarled leather cover and fading gold emblem replied in the histories of the marks and stains upon it and the scrapes and scuffs of storms weathered and mountains scaled.

*I'll need something to eat... water... a bag.*

Carrying the book so brazenly would be foolish too. The GLAS enjoyed confiscating and burning books — anything not condoned by Emlok. First, since the last story was such a swift read, he would have another. Yes... to judge if the risk of smuggling were justified.

*Here is an outlandish tale. Even more perturbing are the events leading up to the discovery of it. I was tracing the coast, travelling the Scorches with a band of traders bound for the Gulping Sea. They spoke of shipping still leaving the port city of Bail. The last free port in the territories. How long this will remain so, I cannot be certain.*

*We met after I had barely made it over the mountain pass to Fisk. I discovered this village deserted. The cottages abandoned. Within them, where I explored in a vain search for life, were scattered crystal shards as though some globe had been smashed. This aspect meant nothing at the time until I came to Kald and found much of the same... crystal shards scattered all about.*

*The next village along, Trae, bore a little more luck in terms of life. A caravan was camped amidst the abandoned buildings of the fishing village. Here, were the traders I was to take in with for the remaining journey north-east. They had a new name for the Draiochtarian Coast: the Ghost Coast. Unimaginative, I know, yet very fitting. I inquired with the caravan leader as to whether this was a result of the Cataclysm so long ago. Her wide eyes and grim features expressed otherwise. She would not give voice to her suppositions, however.*

*Only when her people grew bold on ale around a fire was I able to glean a hint of the truth and when pressed and loosened further with mead they spoke of the object the caravan leader, Martia, had discovered. A globe she never loosed. I had presumed it to be a long-owned artifact upon our meeting. It was a bizarre object and an equally bizarre tale.*

*The caravan had been resting and Martia had gone into the woods to relieve herself and discovered the remains of some ancient hermit recluse cross-legged under the shade of a sprawling pine. By all accounts, though I am sure her people have embellished the tale, the figure was skeletal. Nought but rags and bones and that sphere resting in their palms as if their empty gaze still meditated upon it. Almost as if, some said, that previous owner had forsaken all else and starved gazing into their treasure.*

*Naturally, Martia took the sphere and upon touching it saw many things. Not just saw either, but heard and felt and sensed and smelt. Moving images and perhaps memories sealed in this sphere. The following tale was constructed from notes taken over several of these campfire stories. Remembrances and recollections of Martia's people and piecemeal accounts she passed onto them in supposed confidence. They mentioned too, and I witnessed this, that she had taken to spending most her time with that sphere, even neglecting the customary evening by the fire. No longer sharing ale talk, nor song, nor simple company.*

# ALL IS IN THE ORBINALL

'An outsider! Here?' muttered Edith in astonishment. Her cheeks blossomed and lips tautened. The simple event of some stranger in the village was both worthy of suspicion and a good chinwag. The advantage of being the landlady of the only tavern within a safe and comfortable walk reliably saw that such juicy rumours came directly to Edith. Which suited her just fine. She could remain in her cosy tavern safe and sound. Which was just fine by her too.

The village of Ensum was contentedly isolated. It saw enough bounty from the sea and modest farmland on its borders to sustain it. It had a naturally sheltered harbour in Sandback Bay. The land there sloped mildly to the water's edge and the incessant storms blustering in from the Anokas Sea were snuffed of their merciless vigour by the bay's crescent shape.

'Well, who'd ever heard of the likes of it?' said

Edith with an indignant huff as she streaked the dark wood counter with a damp cloth that smelt of an unhealthy concoction of ale and stagnant gutter water. She leant herself up against the bar on a broad beer-keg-toting forearm to pay attention with both ears.

Not once had Edith in all her long years garnered the compulsion to set foot beyond Ensum's borders. Why, she would be snapped up by foul-smelling Midites skulking down from the wind-whipped mountains sniffing about for fresh meat. Or worse, bewitched by wicked spirits and driven quite mad should she even take in but the faintest breath of the fetid air lingering along the boundaries of the cursed Drakeswood. At least that was what old Ensum folk stoutly declared.

'They says this here outlander come in t'village atop one of them there mekaniteknical thingamies,' said Wilb, a mainstay of the Hogs Trotter. Spluttering gossip through ale-moistened lips was his customary manner.

'Mekaniteknical you say?' Edith said, prompting the old fisherman along in his tellings.

'Aye, I do say.' Wilb supped more ale.

His rosacea nose glowed crossly as if affronted by the mere inkling that the ale supply might dry up some time soon. Wilb was a squat old man. A man once accustomed to a life of hard graft at sea. Evidenced by ruddy, seasoned cheeks and a scrubby weather-beaten beard. Nowadays though, he spent his diminishing time propping up the bar decanting ale after ale into a mouth free and eager to have people hear it spin yarn after yarn.

'Top us up, would you Edith?' he said, clunking his tankard on the counter.

She obliged and no sooner had Edith placed the overflowing tankard down did he whisk it to eager lips. Wilb supped the foamy cap from his ale noisily. The obnoxious sound cut through the dull muttering of the tavern.

Edith and the cantankerous Wilb, who were virtually furniture there, would often have private conversations at a level that was anything but private. It made earwigging effortless for any would-be eavesdroppers and provided no end of entertainment.

Had they actually been furniture, Edith always imagined herself as one of those soft upholstered armchairs with the pretty floral weavings. Wilb most certainly would have been a gnarled beer-soaked barrel. Precisely like the ones Edith had about the place as tables.

As usual, during one of Wilb's accounts, Edith instinctively saw her work-hungry hands were ever occupied. Presently, they dried wooden flagons with a grubby cloth dreadfully in need of slinging. And, when the occasion called for it, she topped up Wilb's ghastly flagon as he recounted the day's scandals.

Edith had purposefully mislaid that blasted ugly thing once — and only once — much to Wilb's implacable grumpiness. He had carved the monstrosity himself in the likeness of a snarling vuvek baring flesh-piercing fangs. The horrid receptacle gave her the heebie-jeebies fiercer than Drakeswood.

'What was I saying?' belched Wilb.

'Mekaniteknical thingamies...' prompted Edith.

Filling Wilb with ale was not unlike fuelling one of those mekaniteknical thingamabobs. Pouring beer in one end rather than shovelling in coal. Hot air came out of both just the same. That was just fine and dandy with Edith too. The steamier the embellishments the better.

Such raucous tellings ensured the Hogs Trotter remained full of patrons. Not that they had elsewhere to go. When Wilb had worked the sea and spent less time in the tavern, daytimes had been agonizingly quiet. What could she say? The old barnacle had the gift of the gab.

True enough, coin rarely passed from Wilb's wind-whittled fingers for most of what he guzzled, but that was no bother to Edith. By and large, ale was the old sea-hound's income and gossip his trade.

'Yep, yep. Creepy crawling in t'village like some wicked insect, that thing.' Wilb prattled and gesticulated passionately as he spoke. 'Legs! Legs it had. Surprised you ain't heard already. Everybody sinnit, I say. Everybody.'

He scanned the tavern, eyes smiling at nods from those gaping and gawping in anticipation of his tellings.

Of course, Edith hadn't clapped eyes on it. She was forever in the warmth of the tavern amidst the time-soaked whiff of ale and homely cooking. Nor was it likely that Old Mrs. Bramble had seen it either. Bramble's bakery being the only real competitor to the Hogs Trotter in Ensum village. And Mrs. Bramble being Edith's other source of gossip.

Like her, Mrs. Bramble rarely ventured out, what with her ovens and stoves on the go day and night. The tavern always saw more patrons though, on account of the ale, Edith imagined. There were nout like ale to lure folk in and make them pliable to purchasing even more of the stuff. Lucratively addictive was ale.

Taking another good slug of his brew, Wilb prepared to divulge the spicier part of his tale now he had managed to catch the interest of most folk. He wiped foam from his hedge-like beard and fox-tail moustache with his forearm before he continued.

'Yep. Lots of contraptions that fellow had, I tell you. The oddest convoluted things you ever seen. But none so queer as what he had strapped to the back of that creepy-crawling wagon of his.'

There was a dramatic, decisive pause as Wilb supped from his snarling flagon yet again. He looked askance from beneath wild scrubby eyebrows. His eyes sparkled in anticipation of his cue.

'And what, pray tell, was that?' said Edith, playing her part. She judged by Wilb's enthused intake of breath she was playing it well.

'Ah, now you see... that's just it, ain't it?' he said, leaning low to the tankard in his double-handed grasp as if it was a crystal seeing-ball.

The entire tavern leaned with him.

'No one knows.'

He straightened up rather snappishly, grinning at the ravenous expectation in everyone's eyes. The wide mouths, quivering for more tantalising information.

'It were big and round, I'd say,' he drew the shape of it in the thick tobacco smoke hanging in the air with a gnarled finger, 'like a rock or stone. Only it weren't none of them, you know?'

No. She didn't know. How could she? Edith was so impatient for more details she nearly cracked the tankard she was wiping with her strong meat cleaving, dough pounding hands. Wilb eased back on his stool, one arm resting on the counter. He patted down the pockets of his patched-up tunic producing his tobacco and pipe and proceeded to stock it. It was a sign for others to speak, to offer their thoughts.

Edith peered out from behind the bar thoughtfully through the pipe and wood smoke gazing at nothing in particular. Her hands were now wiping battered metal plates after determining it a safer activity than wooden flagons. Her mind was on that outlandish fellow of Wilb's story and the rounded rock that weren't a rock.

Everyone in the place had been so disposed either to their own thinking or nattering that not one of them had noticed the old oak door crack and groan open and the wiry figure spider silently in, receding into the shadows.

Not until they spoke.

'I call it an Orbinall.'

All eyes lifted off Wilb and came to rest on the gloomy snug as though the whole tavern were some single, many-eyed creature. Hugely irregular this stranger's voice was and outlandish to Edith's ears.

'And you are most welcome to come and see it,' continued the outsider in an eloquent and unfamiliar manner.

For all Edith knew, the gentleman could have come from some far-flung city in the realm, just the other side of Drakeswood or back in the other direction along the lethal crumbling cliffs from Trae or Kald. Though Edith very much doubted that as she knew by word of mouth the residents of Kald were fisherfolk just like the people of Ensum.

And this stretched-out fella; no way he were fisherfolk. Not with them snow-white hands what looked as soft as freshly risen dough and that delicate sumptuous clothing.

*Ain't seen a hard day's work in his life, I'd bet,* thought Edith as she regarded this fellow inwardly with suspicion, yet outwardly with the warm good-natured disposition and affability of a landlady who knew her trade well.

'What will the new gentleman be drinking then?' Edith asked all hoppy and poppy.

'A herbal tea infusion, if you will.'

'Don't do tea I'm afraid,' she said, as kindly as she could without seeming rude. *What in Seodan is a herbal tea infusion?* 'Ale's what we've got and alls we've got.'

'What about Old Man Klenton's hooch?' came

a raspy voice from someone who had probably supped the very stuff once too often.

'That rotgut?' balked Edith, 'you want to kill the new fella George? You do know what ended Old Man Klenton, don't you?'

'Thought it were one of your pies,' chuckled Wilb with a smirk. Edith glowered and wagged her finger as they shared a laugh.

It was then, in the visitor's contemplative silence, Edith noticed the other patrons still staring at the newcomer, slack-jawed, eyes glazed. She coughed and dropped the plate she was holding. It rang on the counter spinning like a coin, snapping them all out of their stupor. Chatting started up, tentative at first, rising at a steady pace until the usual nattering had re-established itself.

'Then,' said the stranger after much thought as he rose from his seat and stepped into the light, 'in absence of tea and not wishing to test one's constitution with the local poteen, I will graciously decline and bid a good evening to you all.'

The slender man snatched the tall hat perched upon his crown and swooped it in an overzealous bow with all the grace of someone schooled and raised in luxurious ways. City ways.

He was clad in an intricately embroidered silken waistcoat which embraced a severe ribcage in amethyst hues. What seemed leagues of exceptionally black lavish material clung to slender legs that would not have been misplaced on one of those giant arachnoids that cloistered in the nooks and crannies of the westward cliffs. His impossibly night-black beard dipped like a serpent's tongue, almost licking the flagstones as he bowed.

The stranger rose in an unworldly fashion, like a child's push-thumb puppet, to stand proud once more. He returned his hat to its spot and delicately twirled his great curling moustache.

Edith couldn't help but feel a tad common and under schooled in such a presence. What with her rough manner and plain attire. She was wearing an old pinafore she surely should have swapped for something less fire scorched by now. Edith was certain she had memories of her apron being white once upon a time too.

She fussed her hair self-consciously. When was the last time she had taken care of it? The Hogs Trotter always had come first.

'Before I take leave,' the slender man's words were saccharine, his mannerisms as smooth as the finest silk, 'I must introduce myself — for that, I confess, is the sole objective of my visit.'

Another hush consumed the tavern.

He adjusted a plum-coloured flowery bundle of

material around his neck. Edith had not seen the likes of such peculiar neckwear before. *City fashion most like*, she thought with distain and coughed impatiently for the stranger to get on with it.

Folk were less inclined to drink whilst gawping, and if folk weren't drinking, they weren't spending coin. Edith knew a performance when she saw one too, having spent enough time around Wilb.

'The name is Zoran. I have come to bestow upon your village a truly and marvellously extravagant gift.'

'A gift you says. How about that?' said Wilb, following the comment with a long draught of ale and an interested squint of his good eye.

Zoran smirked so his slicked moustache curled like the whiskers of a cat fixing on a mouse.

'To know such things, I intreat you to my store five sun ups from now. Spread the word!' He then raised his voice to an excited pitch which saw silence to any straggling conversations. 'Zoran's enrapturing wares are here for one and all, and for all at an inconceivably sensible price I might add.'

'A salesman, eh?' croaked George.

'You'll be hard pressed to flog anything round here. We don't crave much round these parts,' said Wilb, turning to the bar and a topping up, interest waning.

"Cept ale,' muttered Edith with a hint of protectiveness.

Zoran's grin grew into something sinister. 'Oh, wait until you see what I have to offer.'

There was something in the way he uttered those words that sat uncomfortably with Edith. Her landlady senses prickled and that tickle on the tip of her pumpkin nose danced like fairy feet threatening to tap out a sneeze.

The outsider stooped to bow once more and, with gracious steps that seemed to paint his presence across the slates, exited the tavern to the din of astonished chin-wagging.


The fishing village of Ensum was squeezed in between the eternally storm-ridden Anokas Sea and the ancient Keeraksha mountain range where clans of stinking feral Midites prowled in hope of snatching anyone daft enough not to heed local caution and lore. And if that wasn't enough — which it absolutely was for Edith — the dank spirit-infested Drakeswood lingered to the East and, to the West, the Draiochtarian Coast wound along perilous cliffs. Yep, Edith reassured herself, visitors were rare.

They were also unwelcome.

There were of course the limited interactions

with Stoum traders who interrupted their voyages along the coast on their way to Hain where they would end their journey to make port at Skipping Docks to earn their coin. Though, they never tarried long in Ensum.

There was nothing to linger for.

A fact that brought a certain ease to Edith. Since she was young, she had been shy of change. Encouraged to fear it even. Things were always better left as you found them. At least that was what her dear departed mother and father used to profess.

One sevensweep passed in much the way they always did in Ensum. Gossip prevailed, wild and unbridled. Ensum folk made a vocation of knowing each other's doings, comings, goings and thinkings. No stone unturned, no mystery left unsolved. Today was no different — mutterings of Zoran's wonderful wares buzzed from lip to ear.

Charming Orbinalls for one and all.

To begin with, Edith had no inkling nor concern for what these Orbinalls were or what they did. Not at least until one evening several sun ups and downs after the unveiling of Zoran's store. By Wilb's vigorous accounts it had all occurred to a fanfare pumped out by some outrageous steam powered contraption that did the work of a whole ensemble of musicians. After all the whiz-bangs and fizzy-pops and all kinds of other nameless racket, to which fireworks spattered and crackled, Zoran had gifted a chosen few with pretty orbs.

When the fuss and palaver had died down that eve, Edith finally succumbed to her curiosity and inquired as to what these odd little orbs, which had crept their way into the Hogs Trotter, actually were.

'Yes, yes. An Orbinall. I know what it's *called* my dear, but what does it *do*?' she asked Alba, the weaver's daughter.

Alba rolled the perfect sphere around in dexterous fingers that knew only of the tactile work of weaving. She seemed spellbound by the shape and smoothness of the glassy globe. It did shine and glow in a somewhat pleasing manner, Edith noted, like a green ember.

'Isn't it a beauty?' said Alba, eyes fixed on it. Edith wrinkled her nose in offense of young Alba's trance.

'Yes, yes. Very nice. But come now child. Snap out of it and tell me. What's it for?'

'Well, you know. Everybody knows,' said Alba, deliberately as if Edith were too old to understand something so complicated despite herself having only discovered it but a few days ago.

'Haven't you heard?' Again, in a tone which implied Edith should have already. Edith shook her head and folded her arms, remaining in exasperated silence. 'Look,' said Alba, casting her hand over the Orbinall as if gently brushing the angel-soft hair on a baby's crown, 'all is in the orb.'

Edith peered into the sphere nestled harmlessly in Alba's delicate grasp. The crystal ball pulsed a sickly-sweet cloudy green. Suddenly, it blossomed to life with seeings. Some were a mystery to Edith but others drew some faint recognition.

They seemed like frozen moments, captured instances. Paintings of people and places around the village. Several of Mrs. Bramble's baked goods. One was the front of Zoran's store which Edith gathered from the lavishly gilded board daubed with elegant calligraphy of a master's hand. It seemed captured in the middle of prancing up and down the cobbles on mekaniteknical legs.

'What *are* they?' Edith asked, unapologetically awestruck.

Edith's captivation delighted Alba who explained with a flourish of pride, if not repetitively, that all was in the orb. Everything a person witnessed in a day would be captured within it in a blink of the eyes. And it didn't stop there... Anyone with an Orbinall could transmit their seeings to another so long as they too possessed an Orbinall.

'Luca saw this one,' said Alba, tweaking the orb with finger and thumb growing the current seeing so much so that the others were pushed aside and cast to some other place Edith couldn't figure.

Just where did they go? Edith looked behind the Orbinall as if trying to catch the images falling out the other side.

'And this was seen by Jona, and this one by Isak and this...'

Seeing after seeing, Alba flicked through them all with such rapidity Edith felt as though her very eyes would roll out of her skull. She held up her hands and laughed apprehensively, feeling a little giddy.

'Well, ain't that a thing?'

Edith waddled off back to the bar to serve Wilb who had begun impatiently tapping the counter with thick fingers. He remained silent and tight-lipped until his ale came to him in his ghastly flagon.

Normally, Wilb's tip-tapping frayed Edith's nerves, but this evening, quite frankly, she was eager for the excuse to leave Alba to it. That orbin-whatever-it-was, was truly nauseating.


The ale sloshed into the tankard like a waterfall. So loud. So deafening. It seemed the only sound in existence in the noiseless tavern. A graveyard hush had engulfed the Hogs Trotter recently. Not even a moonsweep had gone by. It was all that Zoran's fault. Edith was in two minds of serving him up a harsh word or two. Yet, it hadn't really hampered business so much as *enriched* it.

Fortune, in this case, came with the price of relative silence. 'It ain't right,' she complained to Wilb, who nodded sympathetically, 'taverns are places for shouting and laughing. For a good knees-up. Not church quiet. Not coughing quiet. Should never be able to hear a person cough, I say. Not in such public places. What will people think?'

Wilb shrugged and with his gaze, led Edith's to rest on her patrons. Each frozen in the glow of their Orbinalls. Edith sighed. She had no words for it. No words at all.

Not only was it the hush, but the strangers too. So many had appeared. In recent days she had been obliged to open up the upstairs which she had once called her own private dwelling. Instead of lying her head down at night in the warmth of her big old bed she had taken to sleeping in the kitchen curled up by the range on a shaggy ardiafskin rug like a wild vuvek.

Outsiders had arrived in their droves. By all accounts, the once still and relatively empty waters of Sandback Bay were now chocked full of tall ships, schooners, clippers and trade vessels. They brought outlanders with their own Orbinalls in their grasps. Eager eyes prepared for new seeings to capture in the orbs they toted.

Edith took the three tankards she had filled and waded through the crowded tavern of silent souls who were standing and sitting here, slouching and sauntering there. Each one in possession of one of those Orbinall thingymabobs. Their fingers walking through each other's seeings and doings.

No longer did a simple green glow illuminate the Hogs Trotter and cast twisted shadows about the place. Now, all the colours of the rainbow glowered hypnotically.

Edith placed the ales down on an old keg that served as a table in front of Jona the stable boy and one of Alba's new friends; an olive-skinned stranger from outside Ensum clad in a sumptuous shawl of gold and wine-coloured red. The three of them, Alba, Jona and the outsider, were perched together on their stools in silence around the barrel with pink, green and blue Orbinalls respectively.

Edith coughed, forcing a mumbled thank you and a brief nod from Jona who simply continued to flick through the misty pictures in his green orb.

'What are you doing?'

'Sharing our seeings,' he muttered.

Jona crouched to regard his tankard, foam

steadily creeping down the side of the aged ale-soaked wood. He blinked a few times, occasionally changing the angle of his head.

Mystified and intrigued at such peculiar behaviour, Edith couldn't hold her tongue any longer. 'What on Seodan are you doing now?'

Jona held up his Orbinall so Edith could see the image of the tankard captured inside. Yet it was different somehow, more appealing. In fact, a rather tasteful picture which caught the light fluffy foam in contrast with the dense oaky overtones of the tankard.

'Ooh, ain't that nice?' said Edith in a flourish of enthralled clucks.

Jona smiled faintly as if the whole thing were nothing. He placed his palm on the orb's curved surface like a Sigikian high-priest blessing a new born child's crown and closed his eyes. Every orb in the tavern flashed suddenly with the seeing of his flagon.

A buzz of approving voices picked up all of a sudden. It was the most life Edith had heard in a while. Patrons and strangers alike demanding more grog compelled Edith to dash to the bar and start pouring ale for patron after patron. Not only those already in the Hogs Trotter either. More came that instant through the hefty oak doors.

Outsiders in all manner of garbs and some speaking tongues she would struggle to choose a name for. Of the folk she did know from fisherfolk's hearsay were the stout seafaring half-men islanders of Rhodethå, the Stoum. There were the charmed reptilian Diraghoni shapeshifters of Aonar that, who, up until now, Edith had thought to be the imaginings of children's tales. And, oh my, was that an Usk?

The immense brutish blue-skinned barbarian was required to bend almost in half to get through the door. He stood now, crooked necked with half his face pressed against the low ceiling, Orbinall in hand waving the image of an ale at Edith. She poured the big fellow a draught of grog which he took between thumb and finger and knocked back in one gulp.

'Again,' he growled, slamming the tankard down on the counter. His tusks glinted wet with ale and his eyes eager for more. Edith turned a glance in the direction of the meagre casks she had out back imagining just how many a single Usk might drain when the tavern door creaked and three more bent their way in, to the astonished remarks of local patrons.

'Oh my,' she whimpered and swallowed hard.


The village of Ensum had transformed into a magnificent place indeed. Teeming with visitors and even a few locals Edith had rarely seen venture out from their cloistered confines. The light of day was brighter than she recollected, the smells too assorted, the breeze too fresh. Yet outside she had been obliged to come.

After a few moonsweeps of madness where the Hogs Trotter had been its busiest, business had abruptly dried up and it was all this Zoran's doing. Of that Edith was unyielding and she would give him a cross word or two.

The shock of what was to come though, she was not prepared for. Ensum had changed. No, it had grown. Edith could have sworn it. Sure, the last time she had tackled the outside world was now a foggy memory but she was damned certain and could have sworn to Sigik it had looked nothing like it did now.

'Not a village anymore,' Edith grumbled under her breath as she hobbled along the street. A street that was by no means empty, which offended her even more.

It was struggle enough for her legs that were accustomed only to the short distance between patrons, the kitchen and the bar. But now, now she was forced to wind this way and that through the humming crowds of outlanders meandering all over the place with their eyes fixed squarely on those blasted orbin-whatchya-macallits.

'Not even looking where they're goin,' Edith muttered in disdain.

The village indeed had more the appearance of a town now. New dwellings had gone up here and there or were still being constructed by armies of masons and carpenters. Some of the old tumbledown cottages had been renewed and appeared quite hospitable. Edith wasn't going to allow that to sway her, though. The old cobbled street too, which she had expected to be customarily empty aside from the odd one or two Ensum folk, bustled with activity.

'This ain't right,' Edith cursed as she huffed along, 'ain't right one bit.'

What she happened upon next was the last straw; a bazar had consumed Ensum. For a moment she stopped dead in the thrum just to take it all in. Rich Salfirin nobility swaggered from one tented stall to another with Simps perched upon their shoulders. The two-handspan-tall creatures were something Edith had never seen in the flesh before. She had heard talk of them enough, though. Sprites from the magical land of Dafadares on the other side of the Keeraksha mountains, often employed by rich Salfirin to translate the tongue of any foreigners they might encounter on their lavish travels.

'Excuse us, excuse us,' came urgent snuffling voices from below, startling Edith's eyes down. A bunch of knee-high folk with the most ghastly star shaped noses were all tangled up in her skirts.

'Well I never! Out, out, you mischievous little things,' she cried, dancing around.

'No need to be rude,' said a rather well-dressed creature in embroidered waistcoat and billowing trousers.

'Indeed,' added another similarly dressed fellow, 'you're the one standing in the middle of the street madam.'

'I live here,' Edith yelled back at them as they tottered away. 'I'm entitled to stand wherever I wants to.'

'Oh, a local,' exclaimed another and with that produced a miniature Orbinall in its tiny hands. The star-nosed creature blinked at Edith a few moments until the Orbinall flashed with her image. 'Much obliged,' said the creature with a bow before it scampered off amidst the legs of the thrumming crowd to catch up with its kin.

'Well, I never,' Edith huffed indignantly.

Not even her own face was hers anymore. That settled it. If there had been any inkling of doubt — which there hadn't — it would have absolutely evaporated right then and there.

Edith rolled up her sleeves, hitched her skirts and set her face in the most stoic scowl she could muster to demonstrate that Edith Prattlebottom of Ensum village meant business and that it was business she was on. She proceeded to plough through the crowd as though it were a wheat field ready for harvesting.

When she finally came to Zoran's store, she found that across the uneven cobbled street could be heard the excited nattering of folk and bustling of bodies as they went in and out of Mrs. Bramble's bakery. She was doing a grand old trade. Edith knew exactly as for why too.

*These blooming Orbinalls.*

Over the past moonsweeps Edith had become accustomed to pretty much the whole village slack-jawed and ogling the bewitching things. At first it had been a boon to the Hogs Trotter, but then there were just too many people. Folk seemed to be multiplying and Edith felt hard pressed to keep up. A recent spate of monstrously large Usk had dried up her last barrel so she was clean out of ale. And without the poor judgement ale brings nobody bought her pies anymore either.

Now Edith knew exactly why.

Orbinalls were glowing with seeings of baked goods so assorted and handsomely depicted in that enchanting way the orbs had of making something so commonplace to appear so appetisingly delightful. They were just too irresistible for anyone *not* to share.

'Herbal tea too. The nerve of it!' Edith muttered as she stood, hands on hips, squinting across the street when gaps in the passing crowds allowed. Through the windows of Mrs. Bramble's bakery, she could see folk sat enjoying cake and drinking herbal tea infusions.

'Selling beverages is my job,' she wittered to herself feeling a blush of envy flush her cheeks. Bakeries were meant for coming and going, not sitting and sipping drinks. Ensum had the Hogs Trotter for that.

And as if that wasn't bad enough. When seeings of her own food did pop up it appeared dour and dismal by comparison. So unsightly that even Edith herself wouldn't dare touch the stuff.

*But that ain't how things are.*

She had implored her patrons. Begged them to see with their actual peepers, not these Orbinamebobs.

Yet no one was hearing her.

What the Orbinalls presented, folk saw as truth, even when the real world demonstrated otherwise. It was ludicrous. So Edith was going to have words with this Zoran. Tell him to pack up. Leave town. She had rehearsed everything she intended to bombard him with that morning as she paced about her empty tavern.

Now right in front of Zoran's door, she stood chewing her bottom lip, clenching and unclenching her fingers working up the courage to confront him.

Orbinalls crowded the windows nestled on a rainbow of velvet cushions. Atop the place, nesting where the chimney of old man Klenton's cottage had once been, like some great green glowing egg of an unimaginably mammoth bird, was an Orbinall. So big it was, that it would have taken two people to bear it in open-stretched arms. In front of the store, that gilded sign of Zoran's pranced and danced up and down, up and down.

'Well then,' Edith pepped herself up, 'it's now or never.'

Edith swaggered along with summoned confidence and a myriad of scathing reprimands turning around her flustered mind. Her lips spoke silently in cadence with the words floating about her head, rehearsing the admonishments.

She drove her way through the congested doorway. Each person she barged past had an orb in their grasp, preoccupied in casting seeings to one another, faces slack and passive.

Edith scowled and huffed through her nose sounding much like Zoran's mechanical crawler she wagered. She cared not one jot. The cheek of them! She was unseen, unheard. Simply unnoticed. That was the other thing that had been plaguing her; nobody seemed to notice anyone unless they possessed an orb. Which pretty much left her and old Wilb who had lately ceased frequenting the Hogs Trotter altogether. The last time Edith had seen him, the old sea-hound had complained that no one wanted to hear him no more.

So, she elbowed her way in, already smashing all those precious Orbinalls of Zoran's in her mind. Perhaps she would fling one upside his head too for good measure. That would learn him for ruining her village.

'Ah! The proprietor of the Hogs Trotter. Edith, isn't it?' came a voice so silken smooth, so otherworldly it had to be Zoran's.

It was how Edith imagined a spider would sound to a fly as it wound a cocoon around it, assuring it that everything would be just fine. Zoran stood behind an obsidian counter decked out in purple and black with that tall hat perched on his head at a jaunty angle. Below the shaded brim his moustache twitched expectantly. About him and around the store, small mekaniteknical spiderlings puffed steam as they tottered around with Orbinalls nestled on their backs from customer to customer. Edith shivered at the sight of the disturbing little contraptions.

'So wonderful of you to finally visit my store. A pleasure,' said Zoran, tipping his hat.

'I won't be buying nothin, thank you,' said Edith trying not to take any notice of the creepy crawling gadgets, 'not seein as your blasted orbinabobs have put me right out of business.'

Edith folded her thick arms across her chest glancing at outsiders perusing Orbinalls of varying sizes and colours paying her no mind. Behind Zoran a kind of net stretched from floor to ceiling looking for all the world like a giant web. Zoran's arachnid assistants crawled up here and clung on there, clutching Orbinalls as though they were shimmering egg sacks.

'Each one has its own marvellous feature,' said Zoran, overlooking Edith's bolshy posture and sweeping his hand over the Orbinalls as if magically commanding her gaze to follow.

And astonishingly enough, even to Edith herself, it did. She saw Zoran see her noting something and, before she could look away, he had traced her gaze to a particularly striking Orbinall in the clutches of a spiderling.

'Ah, my latest creation.'

Edith cursed herself for her weakness.

Zoran glided over to the web, legs working like a spider's and his hands up in front, fingers treading the air with anticipation. He placed his hand beneath the mekaniteknical contraption which seemed to sense his presence somehow, releasing the orb into his waiting palm.

He handled the orb as though it were as light as a dew drop. With devilish dexterity, Zoran twirled it around his hand and up and down his forearm. It appeared for the world as though the orb was alive and moving of its own accord.

So mesmerised was Edith that she felt outside her body, peering down upon the whole scene as if she had died and was now a lingering spirit. Despite the urge to applaud such dexterous feats, Edith remained stern in her countenance and rigid in her stance. She had resumed chewing her bottom lip again.

'I ain't here to purchase none of them trinkets. Nor likely I could afford one neither.'

Her gaze followed Zoran from the web back to his counter where he allowed the orb to roll from his light grasp to the counter top. It came to an unnatural abrupt stop as though it had come against some imperceptible barrier or perhaps wished to go no further.

Curiosity threatened to steal Edith's determination for a second or two until she managed to pry her gaze away.

'I'm out of ale and out of customers because of you and them things.'

She held her lips thin and tight after she spoke. It was the only way to keep her curiosity in check. She could feel her eyes straining against her urge to glance at the orb as though the thing had some power over her.

'I'm sorry to hear of your sudden loss of profit but I don't see how—'

'Them things, I tell you.'

It was pulling her gaze, the orb. Down, down, down. She stabbed an accusing finger at the Orbinall resting impossibly motionless on the polished black counter.

'Folk are seeing things all funny and wrong, like they ain't actually in real life. It's not right.'

'Orbinalls merely enhance life experiences and enable the possessor to share their lives coupled with their emotions in an intimate and meaningful way. Have you seen this particular—'

'Told you once... now I ain't tellin' you for a second time young man.' She wagged an admonishing finger. Zoran's eyes flickered at her chiding words.

Edith dared not glance down at the exquisite orb which now held the most pleasing seeing of the Hogs Trotter. It was a street view with astonishing lighting. The whole place seemed impossibly quaint. She brought her eyes up brusquely, suddenly ashamed for peeking, as if accidently witnessing someone's nakedness.

'I'm here to ask — no, *tell* — you to stop, is all.'

Zoran smiled. A laugh, derisive and condescending, escaped him. 'I am afraid I cannot stop my dear, and with the utmost respect, I do not wish to. Can you not see the joy these little orbs bring?'

Edith regarded the pallid, expressionless faces around her. What on Seodan was he harping on about? Joy? Did the orbs cloud your vision so entirely that you even began to see the world as the orbs saw it? Through some enchanted veil?

Zoran whisked up the orb again and held it so when Edith returned her gaze to meet his she looked directly into it. Seeings of Mrs. Bramble's bakery hovered there. Such striking seeings.

'Delightful, are they not?' said Zoran in that arachnid tone again. 'Place your hand but lightly on the Orbinall and you will know the wonder of my latest advancement in Orbinall abilities.'

It was as if she were divided right then between

giving this troublemaker Zoran a piece of her mind and oooh—

Holding the orb was even more magnificent than she had imagined it could be. Not only could it conjure the most alluring seeings, she could hear the thoughts that went along with them, could sense the emotions of the observer.

The particular seeing she focused upon now — a charming depiction of a pint of ale — had the thought, *Enjoying a lovely pint down the Hogs,* twisting in her mind again and again like a moth in spiralling flight around spellbinding candlelight. But the memory, the vision, whatever it was, felt old and stale.

'Wonderful.' Zoran's voice danced in between the thoughts caught in the seeing. 'Fantastic. Such a delicious sensation Edith, is it not?'

She felt herself nod.

She was aware of the faintest movement and then the seeings and those fluttering words were gone, replaced by Zoran's bone-white face cut in half by that tremendous curling moustache. With the absence of the Orbinall, she picked up on a subtle torment she had not perceived before. Previously the orb had dispersed her concerns but and now it was gone she had the horrid sensation of them creeping back.

Edith snatched for the Orbinall. Zoran withdrew it even further.

'Is it expensive?' she asked, retracting and rubbing her hand as though it were sore from being slapped away.

'Oh, not in the slightest,' said Zoran, twisting his moustache. 'Not one jot. A coin of silver is all.'

The coin was spinning on the counter and Edith was halfway down the hectic street before she comprehended what had transpired. A lingering thought, some nagging thing, nipped at the heels of her memory as she failed to recall why she had even visited Zoran in the first place — other than to purchase an orb that is.

A few moonsweeps later and things were back as they should be by Edith's reckoning. Well, almost exactly. Wilb was sat telling his stories in his usual place at the bar once more. Except now, he thought his tales into an Orbinall. It was the one Edith had convinced him to purchase shortly after she had acquired hers.

Now *everyone* in the village and beyond listened to old Wilb's thinkings, sending him love and laughs and pats on the back through his Orbinall. Wilb had even taken to paying for his ale now that he had coin coming in through sales of his own handcrafted flagons. Why on Seodan anyone actually bought the ugly things was beyond Edith, yet they did.

The Hogs Trotter saw a roaring trade from locals and outsiders, including the mighty Usk who regularly frequented the place after hunting Midites in the mountains. Edith had increased her own brewing activities and employed a few local folk to help keep up with demand. She had taken up importing casks of foreign ales too, which came in by tall ship via Sandback Bay. The day a new ale came to the Hogs Trotter was quite an event. There would be the tasting and naming of the ale and one hell of a knees-up to boot.

Edith was now hurrying, preparing food along with her newly hired kitchen helpers. Sublime dishes. Food that would be exhibited so meticulously on the plate it would merit many sharings. Previous responses had prompted her to update her plates to beautifully glazed ceramic ones she had had imported from the elite Salfirin city of Lor. Edith had spruced up the tavern a little too.

In fact, she found herself making all kinds of additions she had never felt inclined to do before. Her orbinall was to thank for that. Oh, the insight it brought! Thoughts folk never uttered. Edith sometimes wondered if they were even aware they were thinking such things. Did they comprehend that everybody could listen in on them? Did *she* really, for that matter? Edith sometimes came over embarrassed at her own ignorance. But what did it matter? There was no harm in it, was there?

Not all the thoughts that tottered over the orbs were positive though. Folk seemed to argue about all sorts of nonsense these days. Issues that really did not merit the energy. Yet it appeared to Edith that the more absurd the argument, the more people shared it. Folk seemed willing to do just about anything to secure more approval.

For the Hogs Trotter, it meant Edith had to invent new pies and pastries and cunning ways of plating it all up. For others, it was to share seeings of humorous occasions or unfortunate accidents or blunders around the village. Some folk had even taken to staging their own amusing accidents of which Edith did not approve.

Though, Edith did have a fondness for the seeings of cute, fluffy little kotiks with thoughts such as, *Hang in there* and *Believe* floating along with them. She even had a painting made up with, "Never give up" scrawled beneath a determined looking kotik trying to get into a jar of pickles which she had hung in the kitchen to encourage her helpers through busy nights.

Plating up three meals ready to go, Edith paused and felt around in her apron pocket until her fingers found her Orbinall. It did well to keep it close to her she had discovered.

Once, she left it on the counter to go out back and grab a keg of ale. She had come over all woozy in that instant. It only took a couple of occurrences like that before she managed to put two and two together.

Holding the orb in one hand, she angled herself to get a good view of all three plates and blinked rapidly. Straightening, she gazed into the alluring golden hue of her Orbinall until the seeings manifested. Obliterating with decisive swipes the ones which did not satisfy her, she narrowed it down to two seeings and then finally one. Edith sent it on with warm thoughts and *Just serving up a little something...* trailing after it.

She heard a unanimous 'Ooh' from the beyond the bar and sighed with satisfaction as calls for more food came fluttering into her orb. Nobody ordered anything with actual words anymore, but with thoughts and feelings transmitted through the Orbinalls. Some patrons who ordered might not even be in the tavern but out in Ensum somewhere. Edith had had to hire the spritely star-nosed Drowths to deliver food and ale on her behalf.

In a rush of excitement to get the food out and to see to the next orders, Edith fumbled her Orbinall. She could have sworn blind her hand was in her pouch. The orb slid down her apron front before she could correct the action and smashed into crystal shards on the unforgiving stone floor of the overburdened kitchen. A cloud of sour smelling greenish mist came up and quickly vanished.

The jolt she felt inside herself was instant. Such a severe, callous pain. Edith tumbled backwards. She fought to steady herself on the thick cleaver-gnarled butchering table but instead found herself sinking through it. She shrieked as she attempted to bring herself to her feet, falling forward onto all fours. No one heard.

Her hands. Her translucent hands!

She was holding them in front of her face, staring right through them at the far wall where tarnished pots and pans hung on hooks. She swallowed hard, straining to keep the rising panic down but it was no good. She called out to her kitchen helpers but not one of them seemed to even notice her. Edith dashed into the bar in desperation to be seen and heard.

No one saw.

No one looked up to see her and she was pretty certain they wouldn't be able to see her even if they did. As she tumbled forward through folk sitting at tables engrossed in their orbs, through the tables too, she cried out in vain. After what seemed the longest journey for such a short distance,

Edith passed right through the solid oak doors like a ghost and out onto the cobbled street.

It was evening and the street was quieter now but by no means empty. Folk ate street food and chatted. Some stalls were still open to lucky customers looking for a deal. Like a mournful spirit chasing its own corpse in the night, Edith meandered half-drunk with fear, barely in control of her fading body, passing through others all the way to Zoran's store. Her head swam with agonising worries, fits of panic and her own reassurances.

*It will be alright. It will. It will.*

When she arrived, her heart plunged at the sight of the store's windows dark with inactivity. The evening had drawn in and Zoran was certain to have shut up shop. The outsized orb nestled on the roof glowed like a wan pea-green moon. Surely that signalled he was inside, didn't it? Edith prayed it did. Forgetting her aeriform condition, she made to knock the door but instead passed right through it.

Wavering in the darkness, Edith fought to figure out up from down, left from right. Sucking in desperate deep breaths until her vision cleared, she checked her hands in front of her face again but still couldn't see anything. She wanted the dark to be the reason for it. That way she could kid herself she wasn't vanishing at all.

It was then, looking through her hands, she noticed the doorway at the back of the shop. It was closed, but the eerie green light of an Orbinall illustrated its edge clearly. She made towards the door past motionless mekaniteknical spiderlings clustered here and there on the floor and on the webbed netting with their precious inactive Orbinalls. She passed through the solid wood door into a rather drab room bathed in the creepy light to find Zoran sat by the fireplace, eyes closed in a meditative state.

There was no fire set there to cause that glow but on closer inspection, as her eyes adjusted to the scene, Edith could see Zoran was wearing some kind of brass helm. It was from an orb atop this helm that the light issued strongest, casting grim shadows about the place. Edith found herself stepping closer, quietly confident Zoran wouldn't see her or hear her.

*She* couldn't see her.

'Edith,' said Zoran giving her the most principal fright of her life. Her heart clenched and her lungs ceased working for all but a second until she brought herself down from the roughhewn rafters. Zoran's eyes remained closed. 'I know you are there Edith. I sensed what happened.'

'Y-y-you know? How?'

Zoran opened his eyes and visibly adjusted his

mind back into the room as though stepping out of some deep, distinctly lucid dream. 'You see this Orbinall conductor?'

Edith assumed he meant the orb-helm and nodded, then wondered if he could see her or just feel her presence. 'Yes,' she said at length, just in case he hadn't seen her nod.

'It is connected to all the Orbinalls in the village of Ensum through the one upon this very cottage and beyond that to parts of Seodan so far-flung it would take you moonsweeps of travel to arrive there. Every mind is shared through thinkings, seeings and sayings, Edith. So yes, I know.'

She shuffled closer. 'How can this be?'

Zoran raised his hands to his head and removed the brass helm. He shuddered as if the disconnection was a dreadful wrench. 'To explain such things would occupy more time than is suitable for such a late hour.' He cast a gaze at the ground before he stood. Edith sensed that same lingering sorrow again. Like someone trapped perhaps? 'But one thing I can tell you, Edith, is there is no going back.'

Zoran regarded her with pity in his gaze. He gently placed the helm on his chair and wandered to the far wall and took an Orbinall from an inert spiderling clinging to a net much like the one in the store front. He came towards Edith, the orb twisting in his hand as though it loved nothing more than to spin and waltz in his palm. It woke up, flickering to life like golden flame.

'Here,' he said, offering it to her.

She took it and, with relief, sighed heavily as her hand solidified before her. The solidifying feeling crept up her arm until she felt the warmth of her body return, her heart beating, her lungs expanding and contracting.

She was no longer a ghost.

'Take care of that one,' said Zoran. Gone was the silken feel to his speech. He sounded tired. Lost, almost.

Edith began to search her apron for a spare piece of silver. They always found their way in there at some point as she swapped from bar to kitchen all night.

Zoran held up his hand. 'No. There really is no need.'

'You're giving it to me for free?' said Edith, surprised at the sound of her own voice returning.

Zoran laughed softly. 'Nothing is ever truly free, dear Edith. Besides, you are still within your twelve-moonsweep warranty.'

Before Edith could question what "warranty"

meant, Zoran began to speak.

'You have seen, as I once did in my town, the truth of the stranger in your midst; the bringer of the Orbinalls. I cannot allow you to return to the life to which you were accustomed.'

Edith stepped back, suddenly frightened for her life again. Obscenely, she found herself wishing to be a ghost once more. To be able to escape through walls. She also wanted nothing more than to hurl the orb she held at Zoran's head. But she couldn't. She wanted it. No. She *needed* it.

What had he done to her village? To the kind folk here and elsewhere? Conflicted, she clutched her orb tightly to her chest. 'Please, I won't say nothin,' she said, holding up her free hand, ready to stave off an attack.

'No. I know.'

Zoran stepped back and away from her to some dark corner of the room. He stooped low to grab something, something veiled. With a whoosh of silk, he revealed another crystal orb the same size and dimensions as that which presently nestled on his roof, except this one was completely inert having the appearance of a soap bubble.

Edith marvelled at how light such a large object appeared. It floated in his palm despite looking as though it would require both arms to bear.

'I am not in the business of murder, Edith Prattlebottom, so please, be at ease. I am yet to finish this,' he gestured to the orb, 'however, as my predecessor, I have become quite skilled at crafting these orbs. This one is destined for my successor.'

His gaze met Edith's solidly.

The oddest sensation of conflict arose in her. Her stomach fluttered; hairs pricked up on her neck. She chewed her bottom lip. What did he mean by the way he was staring at her, with those eyes that conveyed more than his scant words?

'I cannot depart this place now that my orb is established. I have become rooted to this village, to the minds here. To leave, well, it would disconnect me and that, my dear Edith, is as good as being deceased. I am more a prisoner to the thoughts and emotions conveyed by these orbs and the people connected to them than they are. Yet, for the chain another link must be forged, Edith. It must.'

'But—'

'It nourishes us, Edith. Each one of us.'

'It has you. That thing, it has you,' she said, considering it further. 'You're not in control of it, it's in control of you.'

'As it is you,' said Zoran. 'This however,' he gestured to the inert, incomplete orb, 'this is different, stronger. Its reach is far and wide. Not just this village.'

'There are more places like Ensum is now?'

'Many. Many villages, towns and cities Edith. Soon the whole of Seodan will be linked. Imagine *not* being part of all that. You have suffered the isolation. When you came to me, it was the fear of being deserted — left out in the cold — that conveyed you.'

She hung her head.

Zoran was right. It had been an awful experience. Something she never wanted to face ever again. That she knew deep, deep down. She beheld the inert orb in a fresh light.

'But what about the Hogs Trotter?' she asked with a pang of remorse at the mere idea of abandoning it after all these sweepscores and so much hard work.

The tavern was her life, the child she never had. She had invested so much work in it and, coupled with the powerful reach of the Orbinall. Had become wealthy. Although, all that money seemed like sour fruit without the orb. Without that she would have no fortune, and more importantly, no validation from others. She would cease to exist.

'My dear Edith,' Zoran chuckled softly, 'that is all you are concerned about? Your tavern? Why, with the power of the Orbinall you could open a

Hogs Trotter in every village, town or city you pass through.'

She had never considered that. 'More than one Hogs Trotter, hey?'

'One after the other after the other,' confirmed Zoran.

'Like the links in a chain,' said Edith, allowing the idea to percolate a little more.

'Exactly,' exclaimed Zoran, clicking his fingers. There it was again, Edith noticed, that glimmer in his eyes, just like that first day he had come into the tavern. 'However, I warn you... listen well to these words: choose wisely the location you wish to finally raise the master orb.' Zoran gestured to the inert globe in his hands. 'Once you have established the master orb, you will be forever fixed in that place.'

'Unable to leave?'

Zoran nodded.

'You chose Ensum, why?' asked Edith.

Zoran smiled. A genuine smile, not a sly grin. 'The place reminded me of home,' he replied, with hint of loss and longing.

Edith mulled it over. Zoran's shop and his orbs; how successfully they had transformed Ensum.

'What is it I need to do?'

Zoran inhaled deeply as if he had been relieved of some weighty burden. His eyes formed into halfmoons and for the first time since she had encountered him, Edith suspected she had witnessed a genuine smile from the man.

'And so, it is now as it was for my predecessor,' said Zoran ceremoniously as he turned from her to rest the orb back in its place under its veil. 'The successor discovers themselves. Come, sit. Let us have some herbal tea. I suppose the hour isn't so late after all.'

Easing the great oak door open, Edith stepped within the tavern. It was coming on evening and the place was full of locals. The air was thick with ale, pipe smoke and the aroma of pies baking in the kitchen beyond. The chatter died down — chatter, no doubt, about her — and each and every one turned immediately to see for themselves the stranger who had arrived in their quiet fishing village. Edith smiled and bowed slightly, not as gracefully as Zoran taught, though it was enough. She was cautious not to dislodge the striking fascinator pinned to her voluptuously styled hair.

'A tankard of your finest ale please,' she sang in a schooled accent and tone Zoran had assured her would be strange and alluring to the isolated people of Trae.

She hitched up her delicate silken skirt and perched upon a barstool with an elbow resting on the bar, supped her ale and took in a deep breath whilst waiting for the first question.

'Who are you outsider?' asked a stammering voice from behind a tankard of ale. Edith breathed in through her nose and out through her mouth ready to speak.

'The name is Edith and I'm new in these here parts as you have reckoned correctly. I've come to grant upon your village a proper delightful and spectacular gift.'

A tinkling of stone wiped Yargi's smile to a wide eyed and wide mouthed gawp. The arch. The light had gone out of the day and — now that he was listening and rather than wrapped up in tales — weeping and muttered grunts and the odd shout were now the world's percussive beats. Had the city fallen? Yargi listened, placing the book on the rubble strewn ground. He crawled closer to the foot of the slope. He crept up and suddenly hands and head burst up through the rubble. A wooden head. No, a wooden skull. Jaw hinged on wooden bolts. Eye sockets glowing a misty emerald. It cricked and creaked as it heaved itself up out of the hole it had created.

Yargi shrieked.

He tumbled. He flipped. He cartwheeled. Down the slope like a surprised dung beetle. He flipped from his bruised back to all fours and in mad panic skittered away, fawn-like, mind choked solid with fear.

'What? No, no…'

Noise behind. The thunk of seasoned wood on stone. The silent skeleton puppet creaked and groaned in oaken laments.

'Argh! No…'

Yargi scooted back, kicking himself towards the journal. The skeleton puppet barred the way in.

Yargi's hand fell on the book. The urge to protect it took over. He clasped it close to his chest like a new-born.

*What are you doing? Move!*

An image fell into his mind. A tunnel — the other tunnel, beyond the bowed door... Yargi span. The skeleton puppet swiped, its multifaceted hand missed. Yet, was so close Yargi could feel the magia charge that powered it. The frightful thing was still prone. It dragged its gaunt marionette form along. Truly, it looked like a child's toy with the strings cut. Yet it was not lying in a stranded heap. It heaved itself along. And those eyes... those eyes glared with the magia that animated it.

Yargi dove for the iron bars, book clasped in a bearhug. His shoulder caught the bowed iron-and-wood door and sent a shower of stone and mortar cascading down. He landed in a rough heap. The scraping persisted. The silent skeleton made some unnatural twists and, instead of crouching like the humanoids it had been created to imitate, it distended into a horrific four-legged spine-breaking posture. Its preternatural stare fixed Yargi. Its head cocked. Its jaw ground wooden pegged teeth.

Yargi squealed.

Putting his heel into it, Yargi kicked the base of the door. Mortar and dust waterfalled. The twisted skeleton puppet was several feet too close. He kicked again. A stone shower. The wooden monster was right there. Right up close to him. Yargi gave one last kick again and screamed, 'Come on!'

A reaching arm. A thunder of stone. A hard clout on his head. Black.

Yargi eased himself up, hurting all over. But his head... he rubbed it and promptly whimpered aloud. He covered his mouth with a hand, praying that thing had not heard. His eyes adjusted to the dim light. A pallid light. *Light*? Yargi's attention snapped to the rockfall where he had demolished the iron-and-wood door's hold on the cell arch.

The silent skeleton's head worked twisting side to side casting its magia glow. Its hand worked mechanically opening and closing. Arm outstretched, relentless in its mission to grab Yargi despite being pinned under all that rubble. Yargi jerked backwards powered by yelps.

'No...' he moaned, now aware of his pinned leg beneath the rubble. He stretched forwards, straining to pull away the stones. As he did, the blocks about the wooden puppet, now deprived of their foundations, began to topple away. It strained forward loosening more stone exposing its shoulders.

Digging like a rabbit desperate to escape blood baying hounds, Yargi's fingers, grit-burned and bleeding, worked the rubble away, loosening the hold on his leg and the silent puppet in turn. In one desperate, almost joint-popping tug, Yargi had his leg free and was scrabbling backwards. The mindless skeleton puppet dragged itself through and with a tooth-grinding moan, the entire ceiling suddenly collapsed.

Yargi shunted along on his backside, not stopping this time. *The roof, that–that thing...* He flipped onto his knees, then scooted to his feet and, hugging the book, limped a ragged line down the jailor's tunnel.

At the end of the tunnel Yargi came to a door. Ajar, it promised escape up worn stone steps. Or perhaps he would blunder right into another one of those... things. Was that magia puppet Emlok's new horror he had promised?

Yargi's leg suddenly cried out.

He controlled the faint, sliding his back down the wall, collapsing on weak knees. With a hiss of pain, Yargi straightened out his leg. He glanced from where he had come. No emerald light there. No sounds. No scraping.

Moonlight came down those steps though, light enough to read by. Yes, rest up. Hoping his leg was just a little battered and bruised and simply needed a moment, Yargi eased the journal into his lap and opened it. He thumbed the thick pages to his last spot and found his place.

*Hearing stories of the primordial berganor from the peoples of the steppe filled me with admiration and a sense of bereavement. A welling sorrow for the potential loss of such legend and lore. It is believed, here in the North, that the Cataclysm sent these god-like creatures into a deep slumber. They now rest in the shapes of mountains, icebergs, glaciers hills and drumlins. So they say. I asked of any other creatures of long ago that might be of interest and the name Cnøngnåmgia occurred several times.*

*At first, I thought I had heard a word unique to the steppe peoples, however, after several confusing dialectal conversations, I realised I had discovered a creature known only in the old tongue. So ancient is its lore, and so feared, its name has been preserved in respect not to anger the colossal being, raising it from the profound slumbers of which it is prone. And so, the north-eastern portion of my journey was set: I was to forge a route through the eastern Dusky Mountains. Wild Scorches. Long untamed and forgotten.*

*I was presented maps that did not match my own modern map of Seodan. Towns and villages were missing from my version. Dutifully I duplicated this information, revising my charts.*

*Hunting the story of Cnøngnåmgia was to steer me to a village no longer on the map. Uhgelig, on the coast of the Swallowing Sea. Yet, after an arduous journey through glacial mountain weather, I found nothing but wild wind-ravaged coast. Nevertheless, my modern map did record a village in the Scorches just southwest of the lost village of Uhgelig.*

*The journey along this bleak coast was fraught with vuvek — the most beastly I have ever seen. My fires kept them at bay, however, and I was relieved to witness the primeval fear still dwelt within these beasts. It was in Bont, another strange name for a place, an ancient human word I am told, that I finally resurrected the story of this mysterious Uhgelig and Cnøngnåmgia.*

*For the folk of Bont, some who claim to be descendants of those in the following tale, the name Cnøngnåmgia is unspeakable, instead they ominously use the pronoun it. For purposes of clarity and readability, and for my lack of superstition, I have used the legendary creature's name in full. And so far, no ill has come of it.*

# THE DISTORTING GLASS

Rain scratched at Arbela's window. It was the noise of a thousand rats seeking shelter from the frigid night. Mithering metallic flickering and tapping against imperfect glass, which, when peered through, made her feel as though she was sinking and drowning. From beyond that fragile pane, a winter moon threw languid streamers across her bed. The bubbled glass painted patches of heatless life upon her. Pallid like that of Altilios, the Moon Goddess.

How Arbela prayed on such nights. Squeezed eyes so tight and inched up covers — despite their rough woollen itch — shielding her face wholly as though that would suffice against the night's terrors. The hearth grinned yellow teeth from one corner of the cottage across a frigid expanse of grey slate. No warmth was felt of it. It seemed a gateway for daemons rather than a bringer of comfort. Even old Nanor's snoring, her lips flustering the air, failed to stay that fear.

Each time this night finally came around, as it reliably did every sweepscore, when the wind had sunken to pattering gusts in the thick-leaved trees and the rain was rasping paintbrush strokes of moisture on the window, Arbela would find within herself something akin to bravery. Whilst Nanor slumbered, dreaming of warmer times most like, she would shuck the heat and tenuous security of that scratching blanket and through the draughty distorting glass glimpse to see *it*.

Cnøngnåmgia.

'A tale Arbela is all. Nonsense only children and the feeble minded entertain,' Nanor would say the morning after as she pounded rough spun skirts in sudsy water between curses and wishes for one of those mechanical contraptions that, 'them industologists contrive.' Each sweepscore, the same words, the same bothered look in her eyes.

Arbela and her nanor eked a meagre and cloistered existence, what with Mother and Father gone. Arbela blamed Cnøngnåmgia for robbing her so many callous sweepscores ago after the world had grown icy and molested by tempests in the night.

Moonsweeps ago, Arbela had surrendered her insistence of such history. Had lied when other youngsters pressed her into an answer — if Cnøngnåmgia was real, despite the humiliation of that lie. Defeat was an emotion she felt pitted against the closer to womanhood she grew.

Each night, when the wind sank and the rain grew mild, as it had suddenly become now, she dreamt herself brave, curled her fingers upon the sill and squinted through the distorting glass to gaze that way, to where two mountains met.

She imagined herself out there, the hood of her patched-up cloak against the breath of the night, left hand clutching her mother's amulet around her neck for protection as she whispered pleas to Gastian the protector to keep harm from her whilst she hunted the monster of all monsters.

Arbela found herself fidgeting in bed. Now, her blood seemed afire, her feet craved boots and a trail beneath them. To curb that energy and the desire to fling back the covers and race out the door up the mountain. Arbela set to thinking. Her head filled with all she would need; cloak, boots and warm skirts. Yes, a must. She would have preferred trousers, much easier for such a trek but there were none to be had. No, thick skirts would have to do. She would wear leggings too, even if they itched. A basket also, the one Nanor uses to gather mushrooms and berries. The one Arbela borrowed to collect kindling to feed the ever-insatiable hearth. Yes, perfect. If she returned too late, if the day beat her to the door, she would claim she had gone collecting firewood.

A pang of guilt seized her as she ran through her inventory and planned her lies. A lump of hard cheese and crust of stale bread, some *brusan* too, yes. She would need to eat. It was the first time she had ever stolen from Nanor and it seared her conscience to do such a thing. *I need the energy, it could be a long wait*, she told herself as she lay beneath the covers eavesdropping on the wind and rain.

A panic rose from her toes to her throat. She felt ready. An urgency. She had to go this night, she had to, tonight was *the* night. The very same so many sweepscores ago — the night that monster ripped them away from her.

Arbela swallowed down anxiety, squeezed her eyes shut. Breathing grew heavier. Awareness grew intensely profuse. Her eyes snapped open with a sharp intake of breath and she cursed herself.

*How long was I sleeping? Have I missed the night?*

Pulling down the blanket to expose her face. She felt the still coolness of a place not yet warmed through. The hearth itself still jammed with blackening wood.

*Good. Not long.*

It would take the prudence of shunning her blanket to allow the cool air to keep her eyes open whilst awaiting that deep sleep snore of Nanor's.

A low tone of such regularity and predictability Arbela trusted as a sign of her Nanor's ignorance to all things in the realm of the wakeful.

Such a hush, so sudden and final, Arbela thought herself struck suddenly deaf. She ruffled her blanket softly to check if it were so and heard her hands working against the rough fibres. The fire seemed not to crackle, hiss nor spit. The window not tapped by the skeleton fingers of trees. The rain now dripping memories upon the bubbled window. Even the draught that reliably whispered through the gap in the sill seemed mute.

Terror threatened to grip Arbela there and then. She felt her blanket weighty about her, the woolskin beneath absorbing her like spilt milk on a rug.

*No! Get up.*

She sat up, swung her legs out and stayed there, face set grim and determined. She thought of Father, of Mother. Her hand searched out the amulet resting where her collarbones met. She took it from within her nightdress and gazed upon it.

It was a plain thing really. Of light beaten metal though she knew not which type. Central of the rough circular thing was etched the face of Gastian, blazing eyes of etched light rays and a beard as rough as a storm-swept sea. Around the edge were Gastian glyphs, magia, protective symbols.

She had vague memories of her mother teaching her of such inscriptions and their meanings, like the ones Nanor had scrawled feverishly all about their cottage that night, weeping, crying how it was all too late.

This night, ten sweepscores ago. Arbela's earliest memory.

Arbela doubted the luck her nanor prescribed to such apotropaic scrawling. What else could explain her mother's fate? If the amulet truly were imbued with magia, then she would still be here — they both would, wouldn't they?

Arbela tucked it away, stood and prepared for her night. As quiet as the night rodents that dwelt in the cottage with them, she readied such things. The basket with food and a blanket. Herself, layered like an onion in warm clothes and veiled under a thick cloak. In thievish motions, she slipped the doorlatch and stole into the night.

Nanor wouldn't wake.

Barely was Nanor so in the day, even when she had the sleeves of her tunic rolled up about her elbows as she strangled the dirt out of clothes, beat air into salty dough or thrashed dirt outside their mouldering cottage with a ragged willow broom that had seen better days. All the time humming tunes that should have been glad, yet seemed even more so melancholy.

*Why so excited?* thought Arbela, as she hurried out of Uhgelig. Why would a girl, all of thirteen sweepscores feel such a way, sneaking out when it was neither night nor morning? Those murky hours of the world in which beasts roamed freely, emboldened by the dark. When spirits and daemons rode the winds to torment those foolish enough to leave the confines of dwellings scrawled with apotropaic marks.

Indeed, the distorting glass had spun its illusion. The wind had not dropped as much as Arbela had believed. Perhaps it had been some daemon's trick by which to lure her. The rain too, though not the slashing knives of bitter ice many had grown used to, still came at such an angle no manner of fussing nor tucking her cloak would find respite from it.

The effort had been made. The risk had been taken. Her feet were happy to be moving. A certain wellbeing could be discovered in such brisk strides that stretched the rough track between the cottage and herself.

Soon, the village of Uhgelig slumbered apprehensively at the foot of Mt. Utghar. Forever beneath its steadfast gaze and as Arbela climbed the rise and crested the knoll. She paused with the wind and rain to turn and look out over the undulating waters of the Swallowing Sea.

Now there true monsters dwelt. Tangible fiends like Cnøngnåmgia, perhaps even greater. Sometimes Arbela would linger on the docks crouched behind barrels of fish, listening to sailors endeavouring to shock the village children with grim tales of horrendous encounters.

Beasts like the serpentine Notropheus that strangled ships with its coiled body, dragging them under, drowning all souls. Or worst still, the Blekgøth. She shivered just thinking of it. It reminded her of Cnøngnåmgia, though was much younger if legends could be trusted.

Turning from that melancholy scene, Arbela struck up the trail into Utghar's foothills carrying the imaginings of rotten tentacled sea beasts and fabled titans along with her. Cnøngnåmgia was out there. Beyond that mountain. She just knew it. She would find it and then—

Arbela wasn't sure what would be next. For now, she would stay warm and walk until she reached the copse on the last hill and took rest.

After what seemed too short a while after such a steep climb to the shivering trees, Arbela felt she was made of nothing but ice. Her limbs hinged icicles, her feet blocks, the blood in her veins solid red roads. Her mouth chattered frigid prayers on its own accord. She huddled out of the wind as best she could amidst the scraggy stand of trees. She would rest, just a—

Arbela caught herself before her lids sealed shut for the night, before finding herself awoken by morning light. She fled the copse to take to the slopes of mighty Utghar, cursing the tiredness that stalked her every step.

The cold distant sun, Sigik, wouldn't rise anytime soon. Not properly at least. Some said the sun had grown more distant each passing sweepscore, but Arbela noticed no difference. Perhaps, she considered whilst negotiating the rock-strewn trail, she had been too young to remember kinder days when Sigik seemed to almost nuzzle their world. All she could remember that far back was losing her folks and afterwards — nothing but endless, bitter rushing cold.

She glanced back down the trail.

In the thin moonlight the small copse below seemed harassed by night squalls. Like old fisherfolk huddled up against a windstorm yet too defiant to retreat to a warm hearth. Her hood was down and dragged back. It wouldn't keep up against such wind and the rest of her cloak seemed plucked and tugged by invisible hands, her skirts soaking where they fell, exposed to the slathering rain.

It was grim and nothing like she had seen

through that window, that distorted vision. She considered retreating. But to return the cheese and bread now soaked and her boots muddied and cloak heavy with rain, Nanor would have questions. *Make the punishment worth the trouble*, Arbela told herself as she doggedly tramped up the ragged path.

After a time, the wind cut, impeded by the ridge Arbela was scrambling along. Safely on the lee side, the rain was not so much like daggers in the blackness now and she sought another rest. This time Arbela nibbled rain-dampened cheese and bread like the rats that would huddle in the only safe nook in her cottage thinking they were hidden when it was not the case.

The night stretched out beyond her as far as she knew but Arbela struggled to reckon it with her naked eyes in such a gale. The trail was clear enough, though, and not foreign to her. The boys and girls of the village were no strangers to Utghar, and despite warnings and oaths from parents alike, many visited it. Though not like this.

She felt dangerous and brave and foolish all at once. Wondered what Mother and Father would say. What admonishments Nanor would cast upon her. There would be a scolding and she would be branded a mischief for sure.

Arbela took her waterskin and washed down a

stale lump of bread with some brusan. She winced. The stuff was better hot but beat fetid water that would turn stomachs and bring on fevers. The herbs were sour and the overall taste brackish, yet a certain energy flushed through her. Arbela gazed in the direction of the hazy peak. Not far off now. She stood resolute. She would make it. From there she would see *it* — Cnøngnåmgia.

She was sure now. More certain than she had ever been. No longer was the distorting glass between her and the reality of this frigid world. Arbela of Uhgelig was ready — she would confront Cnøngnåmgia. Would demand from it an answer.

*Why? Why did you take my parents and leave me behind?*

A pitiless wind blew up there on the lofty heights of fang shaped Utghar. Not the largest peak of the land by far. Yet from its craggy summit Arbela could peer out into the soupy night where veils seemed pulled across the land below one moment and teasingly parted the next before the wind once again drew them back as though glancing the land below were something she was personally forbidden.

Then, as if the fickle weather had suddenly reconsidered, as it so often changed direction, the curtain thinned. First revealing the shimmering and blinking jewels in the night above, then the peak upon which she stood. It was broader than Arbela remembered and there, manifesting out of that confusion like a giant stooping raven, the beacon of Utghar. She made for that place should the wind and rain change their minds.

As she did so, she came to a sudden stop, eyes looking out at where once had been misty ambiguity, now was a sea of trees far below, ringed by distant mountains. A horseshoe of which Utghar was the top of the curve and far out in the distance the grey ridges sloped into faint memories.

A crack, much like a tree snapping, echoed out in the cool air. Arbela broke from her dreams and dashed to the modest shelter of the beacon. The shelter was a round loose drystone construction spiralling to a dome. Slight gaps had been left through which the lookout could peer. No one used the beacons now. No lookouts, huddled in woolskins, kept a small cooking fire anymore. War and terror had long been left to legend.

Dumping her basket by the low round entrance, Arbela swept to the slit best positioned to the west — from where the sound had come. Frost glistened in the light of the Moon Goddess, a silver web refracting light. She looked past its beauty, out through the slit over the sea of trees.

A crack. The caw of disturbed birds. The mad clamour of their wings. Cold silence. The creaking, then screaming of trees. Arbela clutched her cloak tight about her with one hand, the other searching out her mother's amulet. She grasped it tight until its thin edges bit into her soft fingers. She imagined blood there, but couldn't pull her eyes from the sea of trees below. The wind picked up again. The canopy, the blackest of greens in the night, swayed. Leaves glinted like the crests of curling ocean breakers in the moonlight.

It rose then, suddenly. Erupting from the trees like a crack of thunder. Above the very spot the sky swirled with a ferocious energy Arbela had never witnessed before. Lightening, fingers of white flame, arched from the sky tracing the rough circle of destruction where it rose.

Cnøngnåmgia!

*It is real.* Her excitement brought her brow to crack against the rough stone. The sharp shock real enough to bring Arbela to her senses.

*It is real*, she thought again, this time dread settling about her. She held her breath. Tightened her lips. Clenched her fists. One about the knot of material, pulling her cloak ever so tight and the other so violently clasping her mother's amulet. Her lips then moved in silent, breathless words. Words of the Moon Goddess. Words to the Great Protector Gastian. She wished to be behind that distorting glass, for it to blot out the world, to soften its severity.

Cnøngnåmgia rose.

Unfolding from sweepscores of slumber beneath the frost-encrusted earth. From its hunched shell-spiked back landslides of soil, rock and tree sloughed off like crumbs swept from a table. Two great arms spread before it raking the earth with webbed tri-clawed hands, tearing up trees. A great crustacean head bent to the storm, finger-like mouth parts opening in a shriek of life. It swallowed a lightning strike. Drank it in.

Arbela swallowed hard, barely believing her eyes. She cursed herself for wishing such a creature into existence. What had she been thinking?

Legends spoke of Cnøngnåmgia. How it was of Jun kind, a colossus of old, a *berganor*. Such giants were mistaken for icebergs and mountains. This was neither, but somehow, she knew it was Cnøngnåmgia. From four slits she took to be its eyes, glowed not the molten fires of deep earth but a sickly ethereal emerald. As it yawned a cavernous mouth, came forth the very same glow and she imagined the core of the creature to be green-water ice. It heaved up four great segmented legs to perch frog-like with finned tail sweeping away pines on the edge of the hollow abscess its bulking mass had left behind.

With widening eyes, Arbela watched as the

creature, fresh from its slumber, stood towering. Insignificant, that was how she felt in that shelter on that peak — even at such a distance. Every detail of it as clear to her as if it were stood right beside her. Arbela prayed. How she prayed through chattering teeth and trembling lips, begging it not to—

Cnøngnåmgia twisted its gaze in her direction.

Intense ice-green eyes levelled with the peak of Utghar and narrowed. The fingers fringing its mouth twitched and quivered so unnaturally Arbela's stomach turned. Again, she sucked in her breath. How could you hear?

'K'tisk thn'ukask'

The voice slithered through the night. A voice of damp clicks, expulsions of gas and hisses of green flame.

'K'tisk nich'akh tuk.'

Cnøngnåmgia, in a few land-spanning steps, strode to the mountain and squatted so the peak nested between its knees. Arbela sensed a foul gaze crawling over her and then it spoke, 'Es'kuk sishk ik dichtukah?' Its voice rattled the mountain and shook loose stones from the shelter.

'Go away. Go away!' screamed Arbela, against the searing rime of its words. Words of language so ancient that it seemed as uncomfortable to her as breathing water. She thought of the village, of Uhgelig. How a better person would have run and warned them. She felt sick, wretched, worthless.

*Are you the forfeit?* The voice needled its way into her mind. Arbela cringed at the sharpness of it, the stabbing, the slicing. As if some knife-like fingers where at her mind, inside her head. Searching.

'What does that mean? I don't understand.'

*Forfeit*, spoke the gargantuan creature, sitting back a little so its hoarfrost glare seemed less invasive. *Souls. I ask for forfeit.*

'Forfeit? For what?' asked Arbela, unfolding from her cloak and finally loosening the grip on her mother's amulet.

*The village*, said Cnøngnåmgia, looking that way with ice and frost. *In my path. For its survival. The village. Your village?*

She nodded then considered how foolish a thing it was to nod when still hidden within the rock hide. Despite herself, Arbela scrambled out the low entrance and stood allowing the wind to tear back her cloak and expose her pale skin to the harsh night and chill of the beast.

It regarded her as a child would look upon a curious insect in its path. *Forfeit. Soul. You?* it repeated. There was only one answer she wanted to give, simply the only one she *could* give.

'No!' she shouted.

*Too old*, came the voice.

Cnøngnåmgia rose immediately off its haunches and set off between Utghar and its sister peak. Arbela's blood was ice in her veins.

The village!

She raced down the track in the moonlight, stumbling, tumbling, sliding and tripping. Her skirts were tattered for sure and her hands grazed and bloody where she had fallen. Forgotten was her childish vengeance upon the creature — whatever that would have been — and now she thought only of Nanor and Uhgelig.

When she came down the hill in the murky night, the great mountainous hulk of Cnøngnåmgia manifested, paused at the edge of the village. Crouched with its back to her, its ice eyes illuminating the thatched cottages in smouldering green.

She traced its twin tail along avoiding the devastation it had left in its wake until she came to the village itself. Everyone was awake. Of course they were. Who could sleep through such an event? There was no need for torches nor fires. All could see well in the putrid light of the colossus. A chatter, lurid and panicked, passed amongst all gathered. Worried glances and horrified curses.

Utterances of prayer to the many gods.

'Please be patient, please wait.' A voice amidst the crowd pleaded. Arbela failed to see who as she pushed through towards it, past folk too frightened to pay her any mind, but she knew it to be the chieftain of the village. A bearded man of solid stock, stout and ever a local of Uhgelig if there was one. When she came to the centre of the crowd, he had his right hand up pleading or halting. Arbela unsure which.

The adults plucked straw from his left hand. Small children and youngsters gawped in confusion. It was a grim affair it seemed. As adults exchanged glances. Arbela noticed not all townsfolk had within their grasp a straw. It was then she saw Nanor, her eyes full of sorrow.

Their gazes met.

There was no disapproving scowl from Nanor, just that ceaseless sorrow and Arbela shivered at the realisation.

*It has come for a child.*

Her mind worked like lightning. She was the oldest of the youngsters. In fact, the only child of thirteen in the village. An age said to be special because of its number, though she had never asked why. All the other children were much younger than her and only those with such children clutched straws.

Before she could protest, before she could warn the other young ones, cry for them to flee, the chieftain withdrew his hand, for it was for the people to wait not the beast, not Cnøngnåmgia.

In the centre of that circle lingered those with their straws. Hands trembling, children no more than five sweepscores clinging to their clothes. Fists opened to reveal their straws. All cried but one pair.

'No!' a mother called. Another, a father began to sob. 'No! You can't have her. My poor Talia, no!' pleaded another as one pair drifted back into the crowd taking with them their child of four pursued by resentful glares. 'Why do they get to keep theirs? It's not fair! It's not fair!'

But the chieftain's lips remained thin and shut. His eyes betrayed many sweepscores of guilt. His haggard face, the lines there, Arbela knew, had been twisted by such acts, such wretched choices. He caught her eyes then, after searching the crowd, and stared at her. She saw into his soul that moment and instead of the sadness she had predicted, she saw relief, selfish relief.

'Wait!' shouted Arbela jumping out into the centre. She cast all a severe look and scrutinised their eyes. Out in the world, looking through air and not the distorted glass of her window behind which she had hidden for so long out of self-pity. She saw the abysmal truth in their souls.

'You aren't sorrowful,' she hissed, 'not really. We see it you know, children, we see through the lies. We see through it! And you!' She turned to the chieftain. '*You*. You have grown old on the souls of children.' She cast a black scowl at him, bunched her fists. For years she had blamed Cnøngnåmgia, but they were the true monsters.

'Quiet Arbela,' shouted one.

'What is she doing?' cursed another.

'She will ruin us. Just like her mother almost—'

'Take heed your words,' hissed the chieftain flushing red even in Cnøngnåmgia's emerald glow. 'She knows not of it.'

'K'tisk ditehk,' thundered Cnøngnåmgia, its gaze shifted to Arbela. A great hand lifted her away despite those cursing to seize her. Up and up, it took her until level with its curious gaze. *I know. Now you know*, it spoke into her mind.

In an instant Abela was consumed by its sight. Her world crystal ice and then black. The taste of sea salt in her mouth and the swell of cold black ocean about her. Arbela knew then she saw through the creature's eyes — its past. Its great migration from delving the depths consuming the very leviathans that would otherwise wreak havoc on Uhgelig's fishermen and the merchant ships. She felt its fruitless search for a mate it could never ever find and she witnessed it crawling from the ocean to take payment in the sweeter souls of humans and finally, bury itself in the forest beyond the mountains to slumber for another ten sweepscores.

The scene shifted, warmed a little.

It was night now, still in the past and all about her a crowd, yet younger, some old faces she had not known and voices, pleading in such tones that Arbela knew they pleaded for their lives. The faces of those about were painted grim and vengeful, jealous and vindictive. The two who pleaded, her mother, she knew by instinct, her father too. The first club came down with a crack, her father cried out in anger and sorrow, yet her mother did not scream. Arbela saw herself as a small sobbing child with frightened, confused eyes. Arbela lurched to save them, to pull them away but they had all the substance of morning mist. She blinked backed tears until her eyes blurred with frosty rivulets and when she wiped them, she beheld Cnøngnåmgia's cool gaze before her.

'Put me down,' she said with the voice of a young woman, a child no more. The colossus did so, placing her before the villagers.

'You resentful, spiteful people. *All* of you! You

knew. All of you knew and some of you—' she couldn't say it, wouldn't say. She had seen in the titanic creature's mind. The villagers, the adults, they had *chosen* to gift children to Cnøngnåmgia. It was not by demand, but by choice.

She sobbed, sniffed it back and set her jaw. She swept her gaze to Nanor and her glare instantly softened. Now she knew. Now they could both share the sorrow Nanor had been protecting her from all these years. That the marks scrawled on their cottage, that magia, that distorting glass window had wiped terrible memories from a young troubled child's mind.

'You can't stop this so much as you can't change the past, none of us can,' said the chieftain. 'I — *we* did it for the good of the village, your mother, she, she threatened our life here. She would have brought—'

'Justice to Uhgelig,' snapped Arbela. 'All this to protect a village? How long? Generations?'

She searched his eyes. She searched the villager's eyes. She saw it to be true. Arbela ground her teeth and turned to crane her head up at the monstrosity that no amount of force could master, but only placate...

'Forfeit,' she said loud and clear. 'What forfeit for the souls of children?'

'Ik jitisk'hatak es'kuk dichtukah ukk ik diusktah,' rumbled the colossus and at that moment she understood its words clear in her own mind.

'Deal,' she said and held out her hand.

The horrendous thing looked bemused by such a minute gesture yet graced it with a colossal webbed hand. Arbela took the very slightest tip of a claw, rough and cold as barnacle encrusted rock and shook on it. She turned to the chieftain and glowered one last time.

'What have you done?' he growled through gritted teeth.

'Come now, come now. Don't bother each other and stop this fuss,' called Arbela looking back down the line in the early morning light at the ruddy cheeks of the little ones trailing like chicks behind a mother hen. Some of the older ones carried those children who couldn't yet walk without aid.

She paused to allow them to pass and told each the town of Bont lay not far along the way and some, those too young to understand, muttered questions of their parents.

Arbela sighed, yet said nothing. There would be no lies, not to the children. One day she would speak the whole truth. Casting back a glance down that trail she imagined the confusion of travellers skirting the Swallowing Sea as they came upon a blank spot where once a village had been protected by a ghastly deal. How the travellers would swear there had been a village there before.

She turned then and would never look back that way again. Arbela would tell the people of Bont that raiders had come over the sea and razed Uhgelig to the ground. Slain all except the children hidden in the sea caves not long after the alarm had sounded. Nanor had advised her in such lies before they parted company — before she had accepted her fate.

'No one will question it,' she had said. It was a common occurrence. She would miss Nanor. But a deal was a deal. 'I too, had my part in it,' Nanor had told her as she wiped tears from ruddy cheeks. 'It's a debt long owed, now go.'

As they came closer to Bont, Nanor's words seemed to fade. Arbela wondered on the creature she had accused of taking her parents. She wondered how old it really was and why it had chosen to listen to a young girl like her.

A thought struck Arbela then, bringing her to a pause. The monster and the chieftain had both dealt in souls, and now, so had she. She shuddered, but not at the chill in the air, for it was warmer today and Sigik was brighter. The long winter was finally dwindling, but why did the ice linger within her? She was a woman now. So why were things not clearer? Why did she feel as though she were still peering through distorting glass?

Arbela was strong, Yargi told himself. She and him would be the same age. Though not now, if this tale were true. Would she still be alive? An old lady perhaps? A crazy notion took over. *I could go and see. Find her, or people that knew her. What a tale that would be.* Yargi flicked to the back of the journal. Apart from a few hastily scribbled notes in Salfirin, there was still room for more. He closed the book and tested his leg.

He winced. It was stiff, but not dead. He had been sat a while. 'Come on leg,' he said, wiggling life back into toes and ankle and knee. Its brother was fine. A little stiff, but not as sore. A few minutes of gentle movement would do it. Yargi opened the book again, checked the moonlit stair and listened.

For now, silence.

He thought how quiet that GLAS puppet had been. He was pretty certain that was what it was. Emlok had a style in which he designed his death devices. He always made them look mean… and fast. Where had it come from? Had it been buried or had it dug its way up? Were there more?

Yargi continued to gently warm his legs back to life as his eyes began to trace the curve of Duyen's mind on paper and worries of silent soldiers transformed into fascination and the compelling desire to read on.

*Magia is gradually being purged from our lands. Again. Rationed and regulated. By approval of Emlok only. Emlok. He who employs the use of his magia-fuelled mekanitek. Hypocrite. Why do people not see it? Why do they swallow his propaganda? Are they blind to the price of this so-called stability he claims to bring to our world? He is destroying all forms of magia he cannot control or harness. We need to rise against him. This is not the first time in Seodan's history that a powerful individual has endeavoured to stamp out or control magia and its users.*

*When I came to the isle simply known as Fish, I had not thought I would discover tales of magia and subversion still in existence so close to Emlok's burgeoning empire. Yet I did. The people of Fish have always been rebellious and Tormo, the main protagonist in the narrative that follows, only strengthened that facet in the people here.*

*Whether a true story or not, only the silent dead could say. This legend is old and the names and spelling of the chief characters are often of hot local debate on Fish, yet the core remains the same. Here is a compilation of the versions I heard whilst circumambulating Fish. I have utilised the most common names which have occurred over the centuries of telling. Names many believe to have genuinely belonged to the characters in this legend.*

# THE UNDOING OF UISDEAN

Scrutinising eyes. Wary eyes. Tormo could feel the old man reading him like a well-thumbed tome. Leafing through an imagined past whilst Tormo fretted beneath his smiling exterior at just how precise the farmer's imaginings would be. It was the sort of penetrating glower that had the power to convince even the most innocent they were guilty of something.

A roving finger explored the man's cavernous nostrils with such autonomy, Tormo considered if the digit indeed possessed more intelligence than its owner. He seemed unaware of its mining for treasure in his left nostril. The nose picking lent a certain uninhibited barbarity to the rough man's glare.

Tormo was all too aware how odd it was for city folk such as his rambling party to be so far abroad. It had taken all his charm and careful storytelling to bring the nosepicker around. On this particular fine summer's eve on the island of Fish, charm took the form of a pig leg.

A conjured meat.

Tormo would not be letting on as to the origin of it though. His fingers deftly fluttering unseen within his tatty old leather shoulder bag. As far as castings went, this one was top notch. It was clear to him the frightful anxiety of being in such close proximity to Creeping Woods kept his mental summoning sharp. It was all about motivation, magia, he had learnt that much.

Holding his breath, he drew the joint forth as if he were unsheathing a mighty sword and presented it to the nose picker. There were only two ways situations such as this usually played out. It went the first way, which, luckily for Tormo and his party, was the way he fancied.

The stout man snatched the joint in his shovel hands with not so much as a question about how such a beastly cut of meat could be drawn from such a modest bag.

'In the barn. With the donkey,' the man barked, with the intonation of a rather boorish dog.

Hairy forearms crisscrossed a barrel chest like two oak beams barring a door. The scowl renewed itself across his brow. One eye twitched mistrust, whilst the other, seemingly unbridled in its motions, lazily meandered from Uisdean, to Tormo, to the cloaked figure just a few paces behind, then to Uisdean and finally coming to rest upon Tormo again.

Grinding pig muck into the dirt with a nervous foot, eager for the rough man to settle and be gone, Tormo stared at his own feet like his life depended on it until the nose-picker snorted like an ill-tempered bull and said, 'Up track. Bear left. Barn's there. Disturb donkey and I'll feed you to pigs.'

Tormo nodded with absolute solemnity and hoped the nod communicated just how sincere he was and he started off that way. He noticed, to his dismay, his giant brute of a sibling, Uisdean, was motionless along with the cloaked figure lingering behind. The rough man had noticed too.

Anxiety seized Tormo by the guts with bony fingers. He dreaded these moments more than any other. The locals on Fish were a superstitious bunch. It was pitchforks and burning torches before you could say Midite fodder.

A clap.

Short and sharp like swatting a gnat. Uisdean, without utterance, obediently yawed round like an oak door on stiff hinges swung by a sudden gust and stumbled towards Tormo as if unaccustomed to walking. His head lolled, arms swung limp, flopping about like wet rope. The raven-cloaked figure glided dutifully after him.

'What's up with that'un?' barked the farmer, rubbing his bristly red moustache with a grimy index finger which seemed now to be released of its digging duties. For a moment, Tormo could only think about germs as that grubby finger ground who-knows-what into the bristles above the man's lips. Germs, his mother had told him as a child, were everywhere.

But the sensation crawling up Tormo's back like a giant centipede was not a dismal fear of germs but a creeping dread that the façade he had so fastidiously composed was about to come crashing down.

'Oh. Him?' Tormo laughed out the words, perhaps a little too affectedly. 'He's terrible on long journeys. Gets fatigued. Never a peep and is as dozy as they come. Been like it since childhood.'

'Not that oaf,' grunted the farmer. 'Him. That'un there. How's he movin' like that?'

Tormo regarded the bleak apparition that appeared to be shadowing his brother with no notable effort nor motion. A form so melancholy it was as if night had become weary of its dark watches and took to travelling the world in the form of some gloomy tourist.

'Oh, *him*. He's incredibly light footed. A better

traveller, but just as taciturn.' The old man raised an eyebrow at that last word. 'Not a natural conversationalist,' Tormo finally shouted back. But the nose picking farmer had already lost interest in Tormo and regained interest in the leg of pork.

Tormo, his brother and the gloomy tourist, dawdled the wagon-rutted track bordered with the lush growth of summer all the way to their shelter for the night. Tormo was thankful for it — Creeping Woods was not the kind of place folk dwelt near without shelter or fire — or both.

The barn was not much to look at. Neglected and tumble-down would have been two kind words too many. It looked as though it had been built by a blind Usk — not generally known for their building prowess — then sat on by Gorgospalt, the mythical giant Midite of beginning times who, legend had it, had flattened out hills and mountains into deserts and plains with his immense arse.

Tormo could smell the donkey even with the barn doors closed. Heaving them open, a disharmony of alarmed wood pigeons flapped out dragging with them tangles of yellow straw. Flies too, lots of them. Waving his hands about his head as if in some long forgotten mad dance, Tormo span round to his brother expecting the worst.

Uisdean was as lacking in motion as a forgotten

slab of meat on a butcher's hook, crawling with flies. Rolling his eyes, Tormo groaned and ensured no one was around before he clapped his hands and rubbed heat into them.

Holding them palms out, a gnat's limb from Uisdean's ashen skin, he summoned a dispell which took effect instantly — to Tormo's astonishment —dispersing the pesky blow flies into the grass-scented summer air to join the other insects enjoying the parched evening.

*Last thing he needs is maggots*, thought Tormo, examining his brother once more to be absolutely positive none persisted. Uisdean's indifference endured. No expression, no comment, no contention. He was dead after all and, Tormo had to admit, much easier to get along with. But he *was* his brother. Brothers looked after each other. So Tormo had attempted, somewhat haphazardly, to change his fate.

He peeked around his brother's oxen bulk at the cloaked figure lingering there like a cloud of flatulence he just could not waft away.

'You can just give up you know,' he said, waggling a finger. The figure didn't answer, would never answer. 'I'll bring him back properly and you'll have wasted your time,' continued Tormo, flapping away a few of the more determined flies.

Focused on the figure and not what he was

doing, Tormo wandered carelessly into the barn. The creak of old wood, the slink of a metal blade and Tormo threw himself down, arms outstretched. Hinderspell was an instantaneous reflex leaping from his mind to catch the scythe which had been hanging above the barn door. It had slipped its wooden pegs and nearly deprived Tormo's body of his head.

Lying there, breathing grateful breaths, Tormo considered what mind would hang a scythe over an entrance. It was just plain asking for trouble. That sort of thing would not happen in the city. Not with the Inspectors of Common Sense keeping a few eyes on things.

'You!' said Tormo, still lying in muck and straw. 'It won't do you any good either. I know you're there.' He coaxed the hinderspell to levitate the scythe down into his waiting hands so he could place it sensibly out of the way.

Dusting himself down, Tormo inspected the barn for other budding perils. The donkey in the far corner began to bray, bucking and kicking, lips curling back over addled teeth as it pitched itself around its stall. Plumes of dust leapt into the stagnant air exposing beams of light stealing in through notches and slits.

Tormo smiled and snorted. 'Nice try. I know it's you Imia. Give up and leave us be already. And call your minion off too. No souls to collect here.' He waved as if shooing a troublesome cat then clapped to encourage Uisdean along. His brother trudged into the barn with the cloaked figure trailing behind. Forever his shadow.

Prodding the straw with an investigating foot for sharp and potentially lethal farming implements, Tormo found only soft summer straw. He threw himself down to rest his sore feet and aching legs. Despite being off them, the sensation of walking remained. Uisdean and Imia's minion, for that was who the gloomy tourist was, hung over him like lugubrious family members mourning the recently deceased.

Tormo folded his hands behind his head linking his fingers and closed his eyes, ignoring the both of them. It had been one uncomfortably long day in an equally unpleasant week. They had left Drakesmouth shortly after his brother died. The thoughtless buffoon had choked to death.

He was always cleaning up after his older brother. There was the time Uisdean had stolen a sizable fish from a monger's basket on Gullet harbour. A veilspell saved their bacon that day or the pursuing men would have seen them both, instead, they mistakenly thought they had charged into the wrong tavern.

Another time, Uisdean had broken his leg

whilst scrumping apples. Tormo took his time luring the bindspell that day to fix the break, hopeful it would teach his wayward brother a lesson. It did not. Though, it did draw puzzlement from city folk who had seen Uisdean limping around in the afternoon like a lame dog only to be walking about with a skip in his step the very next day. After some very quick talk with a few of the more prying folk, Tormo threatened to transmute his brother into a marsh frog. This was not his genuine intention, nor was it possible — but Uisdean was ignorant to such facts. What Uisdean did know was that Tormo was a magiacaster.

And if he were ever caught...

Magia was prohibited across the mainland of Seodan and its surrounding isles. The isle of Fish being no exception. An unappealing and forgettable place, Fish was a tiny fisherfolk's island which made a living off the glut of fish riding the warm currents of the Solnark Sea.

The people of Fish were mostly uninterested in mainlander ways and thinking. Which was why Tormo had worked like a dog for a year to buy passage for him and his brother. Though casting was also forbidden on Fish, folk seemed to care a little less — especially if it helped out a bit. You could never be certain who to trust, though. Emperor Solth had Overseers everywhere.

So, there they had been, on Fish, in Drakesmouth working in a sleepy tavern to make ends come partially together though never truly meeting. And what ragged ends they were... Tormo practised casting on the side when nobody was looking. He wanted to come out, to yell to the world that he had found magia and did not care what others thought of him but knew he would lose his head if he were ever caught, so remained firmly in the magia closet.

Casting, spell weaving, enchantments... every kind of magia was slowly but forcibly being purged from the land. Reviving the dead, even if they were still warm, was possibly *the* worst casting that could be done — even in the world of magiacasters.

It had been a rush job, but with the strong motivation not to lose his brother. Luckily, the casting he had summoned came to him and, even luckier still, no one had witnessed the most forbidden of forbiddens.

On the day his bother would die, the tavern had finally emptied of patrons, mostly fisherfolk, and Tormo had been left to close up. Shortly after he had shooed away the last malingerer, Uisdean came tumbling through the back door into the kitchen sending iron pots skittering loudly around the place, blue in the face, grasping at his throat.

Uisdean died on the kitchen floor before Tormo

could figure out he was choking. He performed a revivespell incantation with poor pronunciation and intonation summoning a weaker casting. What he needed was the shed skin of a festris. Such skin was said to increase a caster's ability to summon and ensnare superior magia. The problem was the festris was an elusive creature and ferocious too. Far too mighty a quarry for somebody of his slight size and jumpy disposition.

They left the very night his brother joined the rare ranks of the undead, along with Imia's minion, who had manifested after the spell had been cast. Since Uisdean was undead, the raven-cloaked soul monger had been deprived of its charge and had been trailing them like a carrion crow ever since.

Impossible to shake was a soul monger, and unnerving company they made too. On several occasions Tormo had forgotten its presence. He had the cold sweat jolted right out of him coming back from bathroom business in the woods at night on more than one occasion.

Yet it was Imia, not the soul monger, who had set the scythe to slip and who had wound the donkey into a rage. Tormo wished he could see her like he could see that soul monger minion of hers. So many had seen a soul monger at some point in their life that their form had become known to all. So, all it took to see one was superstition and a good imagination.

Conjuring a few more possibilities of Imia's likeness in his mind, Tormo drifted to sleep there on the hay. Uisdean and his shadow remained. Useless sentinels, as the cloudless night sky stole the summer heat away.

Embers fluttered like fire moths from the wonky chimney of the nose picker's cottage high into the gem spotted sky like stars themselves as the rough man roasted the joint Tormo had given him. All but a stray ember.

That lonesome burning jewel guided by Imia herself, whirling on a freak gust. Dancing, sailing, spiralling down. And, as Imia would have it, miraculously through a gap in the wooden slats of the barn to finally come to rest on a nice dry thatch of straw.

Dreams of an open fire, roast pork and mead swam around Tormo's dozing mind. Ah, the taste of it, so succulent! And the smell of wood smoke tumbling from the fire. Ah, that smouldering campfire... fire.

'Fire!' yelled Tormo leaping up from the hay as if it were the only word he had ever known. The barn spat and crackled around them. The donkey brayed in earnest, kicking and leaping. Uisdean and his shadow friend remained unresponsive to the furnace flame surging around them. 'Fire!' yelled Tormo again until his face burned with the effort and his mouth ached. It was all he could do as the blaze consumed every spell as they slipped out his ears and fled into the night leaving Tormo blank minded. He scowled and cursed Imia aloud.

'You! You did this. You good for nothing... You won't win I tell you!'

It certainly looked like Imia had won from where he was hopping up and down, stamping out infant flames before they could mature. Uisdean's tunic caught and Tormo tried in desperation to stifle blazes where they leapt up scorching his fingers.

'Oh my... my donkey!' came hooting and hollering from beyond the barn doors. They swung open, embers chasing the hot air out, and through increasing flame and curtains of heat, Tormo watched in miserable frustration as the rough man cowered backwards and ran off shouting and cursing.

The blaze grew around them like blades of yellow grass quivering in a summer storm. Tormo squeezed his head, unable to cast anything. The remaining spells cowering within him were either of no use or too slippery for him to grab. He glanced at Uisdean who remained passive and dumb, then the soul monger with fire shimmering in its usually black eyes, teeth flickering flames.

'Not on your gloomy noggin! You're not taking us both,' vowed Tormo. He closed his eyes, picturing the farmer as he ran panicked and hopeless. Scrunching his eyes tight beyond comfort, he found the spell he was looking for, grabbed it by the tail, yanked it into his mind and cast it with a whisper.

In a fire flash, a volley of thoughts bombarded the man's mind. *Fire, my donkey, stupid youngster, I've left that leg of pork roasting.* Tormo thought for the old man. *Water...*

The old fellow came bumbling back with a bucket of well water a moment later and hurled the contents at the raging barn fire. Tormo spoke the casting, flinging another spell forth and a torrent of water, more than any bucket could contain, came driving out dowsing the barn.

Tormo, Uisdean and the donkey — but not the ethereal soul monger — stood drenched to the bones as cooling wooden beams hissed and blackened hay steamed. Glancing from bucket to barn and back again, the farmer was too mystified by the inexplicability of the water volume to notice Tormo.

His head now in place with the spells safely flown back to roost, Tormo swept a hand through the air and set free another casting. The rough man's jaw slackened, his body became limp, his eyes widened. Tormo knelt to grab his bag and clapped so that Uisdean and Imia's minion followed as they started off.

*Awfully sorry*, thought Tormo, as they walked on by wishing he could fix the barn without attracting undue attention. He also wished he had mastered some kind of forgetting incantation, but they were tricky and if performed badly, downright dangerous. He would never intentionally or unintentionally harm anyone if he could help it.

With this niggling at his conscience, Tormo vanished up the track towards the river Nathar heading northwest for the foothills of the infamous Diraghoni Mountains.

'Creeping Wood at night,' Tormo muttered to no one. 'What are we doing?'


Definitely Usk, thought Tormo as he rubbed the awful night's sleep from sore eyes. Awakened by the smell of cooking, he thought his luck had changed but soon realised it was a band of nomadic Usk. The stink Usk cooking kicked up was unmistakable. He had contemplated sneaking around, but the morning was as clear as spring water and scrawny shrubs and boney trees lining this section of the Nathar river provided little cover.

The fearsome looking Usk, tusk lipped and skin the colour and texture of hardened moss — sometimes even blue, so he had heard — often camped along the Nathar fishing fouling its waters. They were no threat and had not been for an age but to be spotted by an Usk at breakfast time... well that would be that. According to Usk custom they *had to* invite a fellow traveller to join them. Only Usks survived an Usk breakfast.

Succumbing to food poisoning wasn't how Tormo imagined their plight ending. He backtracked a little and turned in the direction of Iomaire's forest. Not a place Tormo had any great ambition to venture into. However, he would rather risk an encounter with a changeling than Usk cuisine. *So long as there is daylight, we will be fine*, he promised himself. Iomaire was a mangy old bear by night but only an old man by day. Old men could be reasoned with.

Casting a backward glance, Tormo peered out across the sparkling Nathar to the lands beyond. Golden seas of wheat and barley undulating in a gentle breeze. In the distance a green Ignion soared on wide reaching wings swooping over crops. First low, then arcing wildly upwards onto the next field dusting the crops with neem oil from great barrels clasped in its mighty arms.

Ignions could also be found in taverns on occasion, in human or Diraghoni form. Bound by law to declare themselves upon entry into any city and every establishment since the treaty. But not all did as they should, sometimes even hiding the talismans identifying them as Ignions, Onrakes or Lairgvrns. Not that anyone had seen a Lairgvrn for centuries, most assumed them to be extinct. Tormo turned his back on the fields, the river Nathar and his travel companions and struck up the trail into Iomaire's forest, hoping Imia would not interfere this morning.

The day trudged on, as did they, through stubborn tangled forest. The path severely overgrown in places, trees strangling out the dwindling light of day, leaning in over them. Just when Tormo felt like giving in and curling up in the pine needles, the path opened up into a clearing. Ahead, in the dusky light, he could just make out a cabin.

The cabin lay nestled by the yawning mouth of a cave. Woodsmoke trailed from a crooked stone chimney and hung low in the encroaching pines. Roasting lamb and the homely aroma of freshly baked bread hooked Tormo's nostrils and enticed his stomach along. His food conjuring was impressive to behold yet completely tasteless. The only person it appeased was his gluttonous brother.

The cabin door opened with a creak and an

old lady with a guimple covering most of her head, stepped out into the tree dappled light of her porch. An ornate wooden pipe hung from her mouth. She took a couple draws on it, puffed smoke from her nostrils and squinted at Tormo with gleaming suspicion.

'Who are you and what do you want?' she croaked, and took another puff on her pipe.

'Tormo and his brother Uisdean of Faroéss,' said Tormo in the heartiest, warmest, most inconspicuous voice he could muster.

'Faroéss? Mainlander hey? What you doing all the way up in Iomaire's place I ask?' She stood square in the doorway now, hands on barrel hips, sucking the life out of her pipe and spouting smoke through her nose.

'We live on Fish. Have done for some years. My brother and I are on a... hiking trip.'

'Ha. A hiking trip you say? Well, I says you're lost. You've missed Raven Dagger Fells by about five mile.' She scrutinised them a few moments longer. 'What's the matter with him? Sprite got his tongue?' She nodded towards Uisdean. 'Never mind, who's the other..? Is that? No, it can't be... Why would...?'

The old lady suddenly grabbed at her chest, breathing deep. She danced around vigorously, checked her pulse and said, 'Well, it's not for me...'

'It?' said Tormo, baffled.

'Yeah. The bony smoky nasty behind you. One of Imia's if I'm not mistaken. It ain't here for me...'

Tormo ruffled his brow in thought.

'When, *warlock*, exactly did your brother die and how?' she asked, rather to the point. Tormo felt faint. Stammering for words, he considered running but Uisdean would never keep up. He looked the old lady up and down, then slumped.

'Please. We mean no harm. I am no warlock, honest. Just a self-taught caster. All I know of casting is from rumour and ragged old books that reek of fish and ale. Please...'

'Calm down boy,' said the old lady. 'Magiacasters are welcome here. Come in. It's getting on and Old Iomaire won't have a warlock and a zombie in his forest.'

'I'm not a warlock and he's not a zombie, he's just...' Tormo thought about it and knowing exactly how stupid he sounded said, 'He's just undead is all. It's temporary. He doesn't bite and he's quite good around people.'

'He's not a biter then, so what? Iomaire won't care none. He's impossible to talk to when he's that big old flea bag,' she said and disappeared into her cabin. 'You like lamb?' she shouted out to him. 'There's enough for two. I assume your brother's appetite has waned somewhat since his doings and I know *that* hasn't even got an appetite, 'cept for souls.'

Tormo perked up a little and made towards the cabin. Before entering, he looked around with a piercing gaze but had no clue as to Imia's many guises. Perhaps this old lady was one of Imia's avatars. Tormo was sure he or she must be around somewhere. Ultimately, the rich scent of lamb won over suspicion.

'Diraghoni Mountains hey?' said the old lady, who had given her name as Eunice before dishing up a hunk of lamb the size of two human heads for her and a petite steak for Tormo. Uisdean and the soul monger watched on vacantly. Tormo imagined his brother's craving and frustration, imprisoned in flesh, unable to command his own body. All Uisdean could do was drool.

'Only one reason a magiacaster and his undead brother would be risking everlasting death in those mountains... you're off to the Cave of Undoing, aren't you?' said Eunice as she eased herself onto her stool, pipe still hanging from her lip.

Tormo raised an eyebrow as he swallowed a dry hunk of meat wishing for mint sauce. He could conjure some but that would be rude... and it would have tasted awful anyhow.

'You know of the cave?' he said, half-choking.

Eunice nodded, took a final pull on her pipe and then smothered it, placing it on the well-worn table top. She placed her hands either side of the huge hunk of lamb, pressing it firmly into the wooden board it rested upon, and bent head first into it tearing strips off. After hardly even chewing a great chunk, she gulped it down and wiped the grease from her lips with the sleeve of her pelice.

'Yuuesss,' she said, belching. 'Of course, I've heard of it. Lived here a *very* long time, heard the stories. You know, plenty die up there. Those who have gone don't usually return. Even old Iomaire sticks to this forest. He don't want no trouble with mountain Midites, or worse things...' The last comment a trailing mutter.

'Midites are extinct, aren't they?' A sudden flush of panic stole Tormo's appetite. Like all children, he had heard gruesome tales of Midites. After the Treaty of Kinds had been drawn up, all races but the Midites had accepted it. They insisted in continuing their people-eating ways and had been hunted to extinction as a result — at least on the mainland anyway.

'Ha,' Eunice snorted, choking on her present mouthful of meat. Tormo didn't know whether to close his eyes and clamp his ears with his hands against the dreadful sight and sound or give her a firm clout on the back. In a few seconds, Tormo's concerns for his host were allayed as she brought up the offending chunk and greedily took a swig of ale from the wooden goblet beside her.

'Midites,' she continued, between spluttering slurps, 'are not extinct. At least, not on this island. But they are particular to their climes. They likes the mountains and the caves in 'em.'

'Even the Cave of Undoing?' Tormo now felt queasy for a different reason. Having to clear a cave infested with Midites was a task he would rather not imagine.

'Perhaps... though they're sensitive to magia. You might be lucky. You've never been up there I take it?'

Tormo shook his head.

'Well,' she said, tearing a hunk of meat free with her bare hands, 'I suppose I *could* be your guide.'

*Why would you do that?* Tormo thought. Nothing was free anywhere on Seodan. Especially guides for the Diraghoni Mountains. He decided to be forthright and asked what she wanted in return. Eunice laughed as if it were obvious.

'To be young again.'

Tormo cast a dismissive wave into the air. 'I told you. I'm no warlock, mage or wizard. I just about managed to keep my brother undead, and still have to keep topping up the magia. It was a mere fluke.'

'Ha! Rubbish. You just lack confidence. Trust me, I know a warlock when I see one. This is the way it is young man; you need to get to the cave to undo your brother's death properly and I need a warlock to undo my years. The cave alone won't work. A magiacaster of some sort is what's needed.'

'There's one other thing,' said Tormo rather hesitantly.

'Oh?'

'I need the shed skin of a festris.'

Eunice choked again and scowled. Tormo was apprehensive. Perhaps he had said something to offend her somehow. She merely smiled in a polite manner and said, 'I know where to find some.'

'You do?' he replied, rather surprised.

She laughed. Wouldn't be much of a guide if I didn't, would I?'

Tormo smiled back and thought. His guts were telling him Eunice had no malevolent intentions, or maybe it was all that dry lamb he had just consumed. He looked to Uisdean who stood loyal by his side, dribbling. 'Okay,' he said. 'But I can't promise anything.'

Eunice simply smiled and swallowed another hunk of lamb without chewing.

The leather-bound book landed with a slam on the table rattling Tormo's empty breakfast plate. Breakfast had been lamb. Just like the evening meal the previous day. It was all Eunice seemed to have about the place.

'You'll be needing that,' she said, turning to open the door allowing crisp morning air to chase away the hum of wood smoke and lamb grease. Tormo regarded the casting book. It was ancient, but in excellent condition.

He ran his palm over the nobly cover, mirror black, shining like obsidian. 'Is this—'

'Lairgvrn skin,' said Eunice flatly. Her eyes drifted to where the cave would be if there were no cabin walls hindering the view.

Tormo began to leaf through the yellowed pages, the cinnamon and wood smoke aroma of aged parchment filled his nostrils. Though the pages were ancient, the beautiful renderings were as vivid as the day they had been etched. 'It's beautiful. How did you come by it?'

'Oh, long ago,' said Eunice, who was now trussed up in a fur-lined chape despite the summer heat that was sure to follow such a crisp morning. 'I'm off out to the next farm to scare up some food for our journey.'

'Sure,' said Tormo, too absorbed in script etched out thousands of years gone by some mysterious enchanted hand to really notice her leaving.

'Twenty pages in. That's the one you want to be memorising,' said Eunice as she left, leaving the door ajar affording Tormo some reading light by which to examine the hefty tome.

Counting twenty in, he spread the book open, smoothing out the pages gently as if they were the finest, most expensive silk. Illustrated at the top of the left-hand page was the cycle of life, except it was in reverse, starting with death. Tormo read down.

It was the same spell more or less. Similar to the one he had used to reanimate his brother. Without the power of the cave's crystals, though, his attempts to permanently attract the spell and persuade it to behave would always be a pale imitation of an accomplished warlock.

The left-hand page detailed the basic incantation and on the right were additional verses depending on the particulars of the subject's condition — injury, old age or death. Tormo practised it all avidly. Again and again while Uisdean and the soul monger stood idly by until Eunice finally returned just as crimson dusk bled into the sky.

Lamb, of course, was for supper. Tormo hardly noticed it. His head was stuck firmly in the casting book as he ate, being careful not to blot the pages with grease. He had already copied the spell onto some parchment he had been saving for something special like this. Tormo had taught himself to write as a child. Copying anything he could get his hands on until one day he understood what he had been writing. It was then he noticed that the spells were written in the Old Tongue of Draíochtaria. The realm now known as Salosnaref. Once famous for its human magiacasters in the old days.

Fortunately for Tormo, he had kept his word-learning secret out of fear of teasing from Uisdean. Tormo eventually became very astute at finding out old papers, scrolls and texts of magia history. Most had been burned. Some of the more sympathetic city scholars had long ago hidden such writings in the vaults under Faroéss Athenaeum mixed in amongst less thrilling reading like financial records and city archives.

That night, in the stuffy meat stinking cabin, Tormo could barely sleep — it was partially heat, partly indigestion and mostly panic. Marching into the Diraghoni Mountains with an ancient lady he had met the day before, an undead sibling and a soul monger must be some kind of ill omen at least. Or maybe even three individual curses.

Which got him to thinking. There, sweating beneath fleeces Eunice had insisted upon burying him under. Tormo was wondering what had happened to Imia. He had seen no trace of her at all. There had been ample chances for some mischief since he had met Eunice, yet none were taken. It seemed odd that the Mother of Souls herself would allow such an opportunity to slip by. Her minion was still present though, which meant she must be close, patiently waiting.

The first day of travel seemed to speed by at a pace which appeared not to tire Tormo of which he was glad. A place to camp was selected, the fire set and their first meal out as a group a pleasant one. But now, in air so frigid and so high up with yet higher to climb, the previous day seemed nothing more than a hazy dream.

They had struck camp as soon as the dawn sun came up over the distant peak of the great Basbuaic Mountain. Up with the morning mist leaving Creeping Crags and the foothills one day behind them. Now, on the afternoon of the second day, Tormo waited patiently by a lichen rich runestone marker for Eunice to make the bend in the rocky trail and finally waddle into sight.

They had made good headway along the Smairsmouth Path, up onto Three Peak Ridge, where Tormo now stood atop the first peak looking north at the lavender hue of the distant but still massive Basbuaic, the largest mountain in the Diraghoni Range.

Sighing, he pulled back his gaze to the mist shrouded blue mountains in the near distance. Most would have seen beauty in that view but all he saw was aching discomfort and sore feet. Ankle twisting, back aching, knee knocking pain. Eunice had insisted she was taking them the quickest way she knew. A route that seemed to not take the ups and downs into account.

They had scaled Creeping Crags only to discover a path at the top trailing back down a gentle slope they could have come up. They had just happened across the Smairsmouth Path taking a sharp ascent up to his present position. A route which would have been fine if they were flying as carrion crows did.

A terrible wheezing caught Tormo's ear, and the familiar aroma of sweet pipe smoke drifted along on a slight breeze. Tormo turned his attention back to the rocky trail to see Eunice, swaddled in so much sheepskin, chewing on her pipe, cheeks red like a slapped backside, drawing herself along with a gnarled oaken staff protesting with each unsteady step.

'Stupid. Stupid way to bloomin' travel. Walking. Ha. Ridiculous!'

'How would you propose we travelled?' called Tormo from above. She waved away his comment and gave no answer.

'Your brother is lagging again young warlock,' said Eunice, thumbing behind her. 'Needs a top up too, I'd say.'

Tormo sighed, shoving himself up from the rune marker. 'Yeah. I'll go and get him,' he said, shambling past Eunice with no enthusiasm at all. Uisdean sure would owe him this time. 'Stop calling me warlock,' called Tormo as he disappeared round the rocky bend. 'It's inaccurate and could get me killed.'


Grumbling to himself as he wandered back down the trail he had *just* toiled up, Tormo considered whether he really did need a guide or not. Sure, it was nice of her to loan him that book. The spell in there was complete and had a few verses the scrappy version he had originally used lacked. But was it *really* worth having to listen to all the moaning?

From the moment they had left the forest right up until now, Eunice griped about this pain, languished about that ache and frequently had to take breaks. She seemed to be leading them on the most up and down route she could imagine too. Tormo was convinced they had walked in a line as straight as an arrow would fly.

Tumbling rocks stole attention from his thoughts and Tormo sighed. He must have finally come across Uisdean. *Probably stuck trying to get over a steep rock or something,* thought Tormo as he rounded a jagged outcrop. Suddenly, his heart leapt and Tormo flung himself back around the crag out of sight. After a few draughts of crisp mountain air, he peeked round the jutting rocks. The stench arrested him then; mountain Midites. And they were close.

Tormo tried to force his trembling body to relax. He could feel the castings leaking out of his ears, floating away again. These Midites were wild. No trappings of men — boots, belts or daggers — a fierce mountain clan probably. All were gathered around Uisdean, poking and prodding him, pushing and shoving each other. He probably confused them. Uisdean looked like a man. Kind of moved like one too. Yet likely smelt... dead.

There was nothing for it but to wait it out and see what happened. No way he could deal with the clan alone. He would get off one casting and be snapped in half by the rest. Flesh stripped from bone, bones ground to meal... that was how the legends went anyhow.

One of the hairier Midites ceased its pushing and shoving. Sniffing the air instead, trying to catch a scent. Tormo wet his finger and stuck it in the air. Upwind. Good. There was little danger of them scenting him and definitely not spotting him. Mountain Midites were said to be terribly near-sighted. Relying mostly on sniffing out any creature foolish enough to wander by. Like Uisdean.

Frozen, part of the rock face himself, Tormo observed something else. A feeling he had not experienced since he met Eunice. It was the sinking feeling that Imia was about to take charge. Tormo cringed as the wind changed. Possibly *the* worst thing that could happen. Then a feeling of spectral hands yanking at his right foot, the one bearing all his weight. It slipped out from under him sending rocks crashing down the trail towards the clan.

Tormo never looked back after Uisdean. Not once. *He is big enough and undead enough to look after himself.* Tormo leapt into the air like a startled marsh frog and bounded up the trail screaming out to Eunice hoping she would hear the warning. Tormo could hear the Midites in pursuit, uncertain as to how many were after him, it certainly *sounded* like the whole bunch.

Striding along, a stone struck Tormo on the ankle, he crumpled slightly, nearly fell but somehow managed to transform the stumble into a magnificent leap clearing a jutting rock. Another stone, bigger this time, struck Tormo in between the shoulders. His world span. He tumbled. He came smack down on his face.

Lying there, knees grazed and bleeding through his woollen brais, Tormo wiped his sore, bleeding hands on his tunic and shook the dizziness from his head. Vision blurring in and out of focus for a few seconds, the stony trail eventually snapped into clarity. *Everything* snapped into clarity. The pain, the aches, the fetid stink of Midite and that awful clogged nose noise they made. Like someone breathing through mucus.

They were close.

He heaved himself up throwing his gaze along the trail to the rune marker. No Eunice. *Good, she got away.* Tormo ran up the sharp climbing path towards the marker hoping there would be somewhere to hide beyond it. A hole to crawl into. A convenient overhang to cower under. Anything. With the scent of human blood to madden them, the Midites were furious in pace and nimble of foot. More than accustomed to mountain tracks. All were almost on top of Tormo when he eventually collapsed at the rune.

The vilest and greatest of the bunch came at him. Hirsute hands reaching ready to throttle. Tormo flung his own less hairy hands up in defence expecting to lose a few fingers but instead felt a downdraught of fresh air, the warm spattering of blood and the flapping of great wings.

Monstrous wings.

Upon opening his eyes, Tormo pressed his aching body into the stone floor overtaken by the urge to dissolve into the grit and grime. *The* biggest Ignion — no, Lairgvrn — he had ever seen hovered above him on updrafts of warm air. The Midite in its talons. It swooped over the ridge pitching the Midite into open air. Already scattering back down the trail, its kin leapt and bounded screeching and yelping.

The glorious Lairgvrn banked and swooped low over Tormo beating up dust and dirt with its broad bat-like wings. It was a black Lairgvrn. Ancient. Grey spines and silver scales spotted its obsidian skin like diamond stars. Tormo continued to watch on astounded as it chased the Midites down the mountain out of sight. He collapsed backwards into a grateful heap lying there for a wild moment admiring the clear sky until a thought set him bolt upright.

Uisdean.

Springing to his feet, ignoring the pain, Tormo glided back down the trail not noticing his feet touching the ground. His journey was brief, the Lairgvrn was winging its way toward him. He fought the instinct to run and hide, reminding himself of the pact Diraghoni kind had made.

It did nothing to rid his body of the heebie-jeebies though. There was nothing quite so terrifying as the sight of a Lairgvrn soaring towards you, eyes glinting like emeralds. It had something grasped in its talons. At first, Tormo thought it to be a Midite. As it grew closer he caught sight of the ever-malingering shadow of the soul monger gliding along and surmised that within the Lairgvrn's grasp was Uisdean. *Why would a Lairgvrn...?*

'No, it can't be...' said Tormo as the creature hovered over him then gently set Uisdean down. It backed up slightly to set itself down, stretching its neck, straightening to let out a sonorous howl, wings stretching so much they creaked like the overburdened sails of a ship in high winds. The call ended in abrupt coughing, evolving into hacking and spluttering. The beast folded in two, clutching its back with one winged claw.

'Are you alright?' said Tormo stepping towards the creature in great concern, imagining how one would go about saving a choking Lairgvrn.

The two-legged sky serpent held its other wing out in a hold-on-a-moment gesture until it finished wheezing and hacking. Once the cacophony ceased, it folded in on itself in a whirl of dark motions, shrinking and contracting until all that remained was a naked little old lady.

'You're welcome,' said Eunice, waddling past him, still clutching her back. 'Now where's my staff... oh, and my clothes?' she muttered, searching around the rune marker.

'You're a Lairgvrn. A fire breather.' said Tormo as he checked Uisdean over. Averting his eyes from Eunice as she dressed.

'Yup. Last of my kind,' she said eventually, now mostly clothed, still rescuing breaths from the air. 'Do you have any water? No matter how much I spit I can't be rid of the taste of Midite,' she said smacking her lips together.

'You're a Lairgvrn,' said Tormo again, as he turned from Uisdean to pass his waterskin. 'Why didn't you say anything?'

'What about?' said Eunice as she took a slug of water.

'You're a Lairgvrn! You're supposed to inform humans about that sort of thing. And why don't you wear a talisman?'

Eunice laughed. 'I know the rules very well thank you. But that's the *Ignion* Pact. As you quite rightly say, I'm a Lairgvrn. Not an Ignion.'

Tormo rolled his eyes. 'Ignion, Lairgvrn, Onrake, festris... what's it matter?'

'It matters to me!' she snapped. 'And I certainly ain't no festris.' She spat.

'Sorry, I—'

Eunice sighed and waved his apology away. 'Ah, forget it. You're young and ignorant. It was ignorance that pretty much killed us all off. It were Ignions who was eating princesses and maidens… and occasionally princes. Though I've heard they're a little too rich.' She shook her head. 'A crime for which we were all doomed to bear the consequences. All because of ignorance.'

Embarrassed at his own ignorance, Tormo considered things a moment in silence. Her remote cabin nestled in the forest by that cave which must have been her lair of course. But why a cabin? He asked her that question and plenty more after they left the rune marker, trapsing along the ragged Three Peak Ridge and up and over Hollow Hill, which was certainly *not* a hill.

'So why do you want to be young again?' said Tormo, regretting the silly question as soon as it had left his lips.

'Ha,' Eunice laughed, 'like most beings that are old Tormo, I miss movement without aches and pain. But most of all, I miss flying… I mean *real* flying. Alls I can manage is the odd bout now and then.'

She finished stuffing her pipe, closed one nostril off with a finger and with a sharp farmer's blow spouted flame. Eunice puffed a few times to get it going then trotted off with a little more lustre than usual. 'Keep up. It's this way, another day or so.'

Tormo looked back to Uisdean, his left arm outstretched, twine around his wrist trailing through the air to Tormo. He gave it a yank and Uisdean started off again, the misty gloomy shadow trailing right behind. Tormo would take no chances now. They were too close to the Cave of Undoing to risk any sillier situations like the Midite incident. It occurred to him then that even dead, his brother still managed to cause trouble.

Flames reached into the night. Amber fingers curling and wavering as they ate the air. Crackling pine scattering glowing ember jewels. The scent of pine needles and woodsmoke filled the air around their little camp. Not long after the Midite incident they had passed a copse of pine. Perpetually thinking of her ravenous appetite, Eunice, had suggested Tormo might want to bundle some firewood to keep mountain wolves and wild Midites at bay. She had mentioned something about a treat for their evening meal too. The thought of a treat intrigued Tormo. It would certainly beat the tasteless stuff he had conjured up for lunch after his castings had fluttered back into his head.

That was the trouble with castings. You could memorise them. Right down to perfecting their pronunciation and rhythm, which was the key to attracting the magia. To coax it from its hiding place out in the world and convince it to remain with you. They were like wild animals, castings. It took time, building up trust. One good fright and they scattered into the world again.

Tormo sighed as he thought and his stomach sighed along with him. Eunice stood. 'Sounds like you're ready for something to eat,' she said, rubbing her hands together. 'How about some roast lamb? Mmm, on an open fire.'

Tormo looked around and saw no lamb. 'You're going to hunt?'

Eunice laughed. 'At night? At my age? Ha! No. That wouldn't be wise.

'I can't do lamb,' said Tormo. 'Uisdean was fonder of pork.' He regarded his brother in the firelight, drooling. He could hear then, probably see everything to. Good. Maybe this whole fiasco would teach him a good lesson.

'No conjuring necessary,' said Eunice tapping her nose. 'Don't have to do this in secret now the spriggan's out of the bag,' she said, and whirled into her fearsome Lairgvrn form. Tormo fought the natural instinct to flee and marvelled instead at how daunting Eunice looked by firelight.

She hacked and hocked and hacked. Tormo winced as Eunice hacked some more and brought up a whole lamb. It slapped wetly on the ground and he nearly threw up. 'What about that?' growled Eunice.

'You want me to eat that?' Tormo made no effort to hide his disgust, a hand over his mouth.

'What?' said Eunice incredulous.

'Where did you even have that? In fact, I'd rather not know. I appreciate the effort, but I'm not eating it.'

'Why ever not?' replied Eunice.

'Germs.'

Eunice laughed, inhaled deeply and spouted flame roasting the lamb in an instant. 'No germs,' she said, folding her wings across her chest as if she were in her human form. It was a day of firsts for Tormo. His first Lairgvrn and then his first smug Lairgvrn. She whirled in on herself and took human form again. 'Right then. That's settled. So stop being a big old fluffy pelice about it and eat.'


Imia let them be that night, leaving the fire unmolested. It was still smouldering when Tormo awoke and rose to untether his brother. The morning evaporated after that and he felt like they had never stopped or even slept. The trail went on and on. Higher and higher along the sweeping curve of Zorgarn's Saddle. The wind would pick up and they would have to slow their pace. It was an arduous and clunky ascent with Uisdean in tow.

It was almost midday when they spotted the figures on the horizon. At first Tormo was concerned to see people so deep in the mountains, but that concern transformed into curiosity as the figures made no discernible movement nor motion. Even as their party came upon them.

'What happened to them?' said Tormo wrapping one of the figures on the head. It rang like solid stone. *A traveller of sorts, but why out here?* He looked along the shale slope down into the basin. Dozens of figures stood against the mountain breeze. Silent onlookers.

'They came for the cave, like you,' said Eunice, scouring the immediate slope and sniffing the air. 'Something very old lives here.'

'What did this?' said Tormo, examining another statue. This time a mountain Midite. Perhaps it had strayed too far from its cave.

'A petrifier,' said Eunice. 'Anguir probably.'

'You know him?'

'*Her*. And yes. I know her.' Eunice seemed saddened, searching the land until she spotted what she was looking for and shuffled down the scree slope.

'Where are you going?' called Tormo, distress in his voice, looking wildly around for this Anguir the Petrifier. Was she crazy? He certainly did not want to be turned to stone. Eunice seemed unperturbed and determined to get wherever she was headed. He followed, winding down the slope and sliding in the scree until they came to a stop and Tormo figured it out.

Eunice stood, weeping softly, one time-knotted hand resting on the stone leg of a small Lairgvrn. The creature frozen forever taking to flight. Tormo laid a hand on her right shoulder hoping she would accept his gesture. 'Your child?'

'Yes,' replied Eunice, wiping away a tear. She sniffed. 'Anguir. She did this. We had settled here to rest our wings — my daughter and I. I had wanted to show her these mountains. Diraghoni. Named after our kind, you know. I wanted her to see these mountains.' She turned into Tormo's chest. He stretched his arm around her. 'I've never forgiven myself.'

Tormo felt struck dumb not knowing what to say. He craned his neck up to regard Eunice's daughter. She was a beautiful example of a young Lairgvrn. Her majestic sail ran from the top of her head tapering down to her spear-tipped tail.

Her wings were held right back as if she were just about to give one mighty push and be off. Lichen dappled her granite body and the details of scales and spines had all but been chipped and worn away by mountain weather.

Eunice straightened and looked past her daughter. 'Come on,' she said. 'The cave is just down this slope.'

Tormo nodded, tugged on his twine and Uisdean lurched along after them, unsteady on the scree. It was hard going. Every step they took they sank. Small stones working their way into his sheep hide shoes rubbing his ankles sore. By the time they had caught sight of the cave entrance in the near distance, Tormo was in agony vowing his next casting to learn would be for a better pair of shoes.

'There,' said Eunice, pointing at the sheer face ahead of them. 'Can you see the markers?'

Squinting the distant cobalt cliffs into clarity, Tormo could just make out the entrance. Though at this distance it looked no bigger than a mousehole. Fired up with a renewing energy he made forward but Eunice held him gently back.

'Careful. You want to end up like them?' she nodded in the direction of the statues. 'She's under the loose scree somewhere. Waiting.'

'Maybe she's dead,' said Tormo with hope.

Eunice laughed. 'Ha! Not her. Not a festris, they live long lives. Magia guards magia Tormo — and viciously so.' She set off trailing the rocky fringe that encircled Anguir's fold. 'Stay on solid rock where you can and don't make a fuss with your feet.'

Tormo glanced at his cumbersome brother and winced. *This is going to be fun*. But there, staring deep into his brother's eyes, Tormo saw something. A change — sorrow.

'Don't worry brother,' said Tormo, directly to Uisdean for the first time since he had postponed his death, 'we'll get there. We'll take it slow.' He tugged gently on the tether and set off after Eunice. The soul monger smiled on, as it always did, waiting for the inevitable.

She was there, somewhere. Anguir slumbered beneath the loose covering of shale. Each step along the sloping edge brought more and more signs that she was there. Great rents in crags and boulders bore the scrawling of her claws. Flakes of skin caught in the rough stone, dry and crisp. Tormo gathered as much as he could, shivering at thoughts of germs.

It was only when Uisdean slipped down to the

shale floor that Tormo felt the cold presence of the soul monger bearing down upon all of them. The monger grinned silently as they all winced. While easing Uisdean back onto the ledge from which he had slipped as quietly as he could, something about the shale caught Tormo's eye. He knelt and took a piece to examine.

'This rock is wearing a ring,' he whispered up to Eunice.

She nodded grimly. 'All this... all you see, Tormo, Anguir bathes eternal in the remains of her enemies.'

He returned the petrified finger gingerly and stepped up from the shale. Features set grim. Jaw rigid with anxiety. He pulled on the tether so Uisdean would follow yet it seemed that Imia was furious that her efforts had been thwarted; the tether came loose at the knot. Tormo fell forward without the bulk of his brother as resistance against his tug. He stumbled, slipped and scrambled for stability and managed to lean into the steep slope and steady himself. It was too late though. His feet had already sent an avalanche of stone skipping and scattering to the basin floor.

A vent of shale suddenly burst into the air showering them all with fine grit and rock. Tormo froze to the spot. Uisdean lumbered on. First stumbling downwards, then falling, then rolling, finally sliding to a face-down stop in the shale basin. Another blast of rock like a geyser erupted, too close this time. The ground rippled with the motions of something obscenely large. Tormo felt his castings leave him — scattering like rabbits evading a fox.

'She's grown,' said Eunice in a dismal tone. She glanced at Tormo for the first time with alarm in her eyes. Hope ebbed from him in the most terrible way leaving behind a hollow emptiness to be filled with dread.

'Whatever happens,' said Eunice, 'you get to the cave.' Another vent of rock and the ground began to sink in on itself filling the void left behind by the great festris rising from beneath. Before Eunice could say anymore the light was blotted out and a shadow so terrible painted itself over them all.

Anguir stood poised on her forelimbs (the only limbs she possessed), half her serpentine form looming high above, the rest slinking back into the shale.

Expanding outwards, growing and growing, Eunice transmogrified into her Lairgvrn form. Tormo felt as heavy as stone for a second or two. No match in stature to Anguir, Eunice nevertheless spread her wings making herself seem so big the festris appeared hesitant at first. Eunice bellowed such a thunderous roar Tormo thought her a thousand years younger. Dumbfounded with no incantation for the stony breath of a festris, he stood in stunned awe just watching.

Anguir reared up hissing then inhaled ready to strike. Eunice let flame immediately with such ferocity and volume the serpent's entire upper body was engulfed in a blossoming fiery rose. She screeched. Leaping forth from the shale like a great sea fish, Anguir dove into the stony cold depths throwing up a shower of shale and fragments of petrified victims as she disappeared.

Folding her wings around her, Eunice held back the shale storm then took to the air in unsteady flight casting flame downwards as Anguir resurfaced right beneath her casting a fog-like breath upwards. Anguir's attempts to petrify Eunice were simply blown in her snarling face with gusting blasts of the Lairgvrn's wings.

Sanity took hold of Tormo as he witnessed the two magia beasts face off. *Why am I still here?* He grabbed Uisdean by the wrist and took off over the shale.

Tormo could feel his legs solidify as Anguir turned her attention to them. His heart turned to stone as the paralysis of impending death took him. The great festris coiled back like a loaded spring, tucking in her forearms and plunged beneath. The ground bore evidence to her movements, tracing a rippling line along, directly towards Tormo glancing over his shoulder in panic.

'Go!' bellowed Eunice as she came down heavily. Weariness and age getting the better of her. Her Lairgvrn voice carried in rolling waves of thunder in what seemed like the stillest day.

Tormo snapped out of his daze and focused on as fast a pace as Uisdean would allow. The ground shook with Anguir's thrashing up and plunging down. Stagnant air came alive with the buffeting wings of Eunice above — revived and in swooping flight. A shadow cast coldness over Tormo. He dared not glance back. Instead, he ploughed ahead intent on his goal praying to any kind deity listening that the shadow was not the festris. The ground trembled beneath him. Anguir's quaking motions unsettling his feet. His lolloping stride became erratic.

A shower of stone and Tormo knew Anguir had broken the surface again. Instead of the rigor mortis inducing breath of stone he expected, a blast heat licked his neck and the smell of singed hair filled his nostrils.

Daring a glance back, he slowed. The serpentine adversaries were intertwined in thrashing battle tackling each other's magia attacks. Anguir seemed impervious yet slightly fearful of fire. Dodging and lashing about as Eunice relentlessly ensured the creature was engulfed in flame. Anguir fought for an opening to cast her petrifying breath. Eunice slashing with claws, her tail whipping.

Glancing back round, Tormo was relieved to see the cave entrance closer. Hope returned with energy to lunge forwards. With all his breath and might, his legs burned and his outstretched arm ached from clutching his brother's wrist. The soul monger hovered effortlessly above. It seemed larger than normal, gloomier too. Tormo worried what that might mean but for a few more minutes until he left the cold light of day and passed into the Cave of Undoing leaving the festris and Lairgvrn to their personal clash.

At a softer pace, Tormo, Uisdean and the soul monger wandered along a rune adorned tunnel. The dwindling daylight cast silver etchings in gleaming stone. Crystal specks shimmered like stars until they were too deep within the mountain for light to venture. Placing his hand within his bag, Tormo drew forth a torch and concentrating as hard as he could, he strained to ignite it. His head ached, his mouth became parched, the skin of his hands became dry to the touch and the torch kindled a flicker at first, then burst into a healthy, hungry flame.

Flickering orange lit the tunnel and Tormo crept down until it opened up into a resplendent crystal chamber — a giant Amethyst geode. Empurpled light rippled in fluid waves dappling the chamber. Central was an altar hewn from quartz-veined granite. Leading his brother, Tormo placed him in the centre commanding him to stay. He stepped back and knelt, retrieving the festris skin. Tormo ground it into a fine powder in his palm and took his waterskin carefully shaking the powder in. He shook it then drank some of the mixture.

The soul monger looked upon *him* now, its eyes gleaming purple light and mouth open in a dry soundless laugh. Tormo frowned but paid no mind. Instead, he looked inward searching for a change though felt nothing. He closed his eyes hoping the rumoured properties of such an elixir were true.

Taking the parchment from his bag, Tormo unrolled the scroll and checked the spell he had duplicated. Pushing away the doubt he had copied it wrong, reassuring himself he was meticulous in such matters, he sucked in a deep breath. Tormo stood, leaving the parchment by his bag and focused on his brother.

The soul monger focused along with him. Shadowing his steps as he moved in closer to Uisdean. Tormo's lips pressed out every plosive, curled around each vowel and breathed out fricatives in intuitive fluidity. His heart flourished in the warmth of magia power. His veins alight with the energy of the chamber. He repeated the verses again and again. The intensity of the power within increased. Each second Tormo felt the magia dwelling in the cavern come a little closer. Now he had it in his grasp. Instinctively, Tormo cast it out in a great sphere of lilac energy.

A sudden drain of life took him by surprise and he fell to his knees not feeling the impact. Opening his eyes, he saw Uisdean shudder with life, his skin flushed a vibrant olive hue once again, his muscles tensed with the fire of life — Tormo's own life.

Collapsed on the floor, Tormo stared up at the amethyst encrusted ceiling until the soul monger obscured his view. It chuckled silently and Tormo knew right then it had been him all along. The monger had trailed all this way for him. It had foreseen the price he would have to pay and in ignorance and haste to save his brother, Tormo had not.

The soul monger turned to smoke before his eyes leaving behind his brother's face staring down on him. He was saying something. Tormo found himself oddly deaf. He tried to reply, but his body was no longer his. Neither was his life force which now resided within Uisdean. Tormo's mind smiled at his own undoing as he drifted along in the wake of the soul monger's flowing cloak of shadows.

\*

Uisdean held one arm up against the light of day as he stumbled out of the Cave of Undoing with Tormo slung over one broad shoulder. The life force he felt was beyond that which he had ever known before. A power passed along with his brother's life force that he had so readily given to him. Awoken was how he felt. Truly awoken.

As his eyes adjusted and the confusion of being alive again left him, he scanned the shale basin for Eunice, the Lairgvrn that had saved him from the Midites. He wanted to thank her, though he feared she had met her match.

Gradually the light of day lost its blinding harshness and brought into focus the dark towering form of the Lairgvrn stood atop the fallen festris. He sighed relief and made his way over to the victorious creature.

Eunice was eating of Anguir when Uisdean arrived. Her muzzle glistened blood. She turned instinctively, swallowed and smiled. 'You made it then,' she said. Then cast her eyes to his shoulder. 'Mmm, I figured as much.'

An anger rose within him. Uisdean frowned. 'You knew this would happen?'

The Lairgvrn nodded. 'I had my suspicions. Your brother was no accomplished warlock. Ignorant of the cost of such forbidden castings. They're forbidden for a reason you know.'

Uisdean snarled. 'You, you knew...'

'Oh, don't get all saintly now, you selfish pig. It's your fault, your guilt. Not mine.' She hopped down from Anguir's body like a crow and stretched her wings. 'The casting took. How do you feel? Full of magia I hope.'

Uisdean felt puzzled by the oddly placed question, as if she had not even noticed he was livid. Then it came to him like some terrible dawn. He lowered his brother's body and began to step backwards. 'The casting book, you—'

'Ate the warlock that had owned it, yes. Bought me several thousand years more that morsel did. He was a powerful one. Much more powerful than your brother. But I shan't complain. The power of the cave no doubt topped up what he lacked.' Eunice grinned, bloody and terrible, stepping towards him. She swooped low, encircling Uisdean, enclosing him in a dreadful curtain of wings. He fell backwards.

'You see, with the ban on magia and my increasing years, it's been tough finding any magia folk these days. And blow me down if one didn't just stroll into my lair.'

She opened her wings to reveal Tormo's lifeless body and craned her head close to it. 'I'll eat him first, just to be certain.' Emerald eyes flashed a malicious arrogance. 'But I'm confident his enhanced magia passed along to you. Ah, you, my dear dessert.'

Scooping up Tormo in her mouth she knocked back her head so he slid down her throat. Uisdean grimaced. Then fury grew within him. A rage he had not felt before as he watched that daemon consume the one person who had cared for him — who had sacrificed his life for *him*. Uisdean. Such a pointless human being. Always causing trouble. Only looking out for himself.

Eunice turned to Uisdean and in an instant scooped him up swallowing him whole. Some luck bestowing deity must have teamed with Imia, however. Uisdean became lodged, not in the Lairgvrn's throat, but her windpipe. The first spasm was a crushing wet embrace as Eunice gagged. Another and another, increasing in strength and rapidity until Uisdean could only assume that his great bulk was choking the beast. Uisdean spread himself as wide as he could, fighting against her body's efforts to dislodge him. Staying solidly put.

She choked and choked.

He felt her hammering at her chest to no avail.

The strength leaving her weak old Lairgvrn body. Uisdean's wet fleshy world fell and the thud of impact rippled through the muscles of the Lairgvrn's throat. Soaked in mucus and stinking Uisdean he smiled. The creature had finally choked to death. He began to claw his way out. It was slippery going and he thought he would suffocate, but rage pulled him along, that and a thought...

He acted fast after he had crawled out of the Lairgvrn's mouth. Finding the sharpest slate he could and locating a gap in Eunice's tough scales to make the incision, Uisdean emptied her stomach of its contents. The stink was awful, but he did not care. A small price to pay to retrieve his brother... but he would have to hurry.

Uncertain as to how long the magia would remain in his own body. Uisdean dragged Tormo out onto the shale and hefted him onto his shoulders an dragged him back to the cave, his mind made up.

His lips began to motion the words he had heard his brother practicing so earnestly to save his life. He needed no parchment to remember. Though, the festris elixir probably wouldn't go amiss. Uisdean just hoped his pronunciation was as decent as his brother's.

He stepped into the cave considering what he had learned; the earnest love of a brother and that you should always — *always* — chew your food. Pausing, Uisdean looked back at the world one more time and made a promise to Imia, the Mother of Souls. *I will set things right. I will restore my brother and accept my own undoing.*

Were these people real? Yargi asked himself, resting the book on his lap. Had such bold folk truly existed in this world? Most folk were scared most of the time these days. Scared, weak and broken — like him. And *summoning* magia? Was it possible? If he could learn, like Tormo, he could...

'Who am I kidding? I'm just a kid,' he said to the book, stroking it as if it were a little frightened bird.

An owl let out a tentative hoot. Then in the silence that followed, started up again. To Yargi the night bird was a tolling bell. *What is your message?* Came the unbidden question and swiftly the answer as bright and conspicuous as the moonlight gilding the steps — the sixth dawn was coming.

'Tomorrow,' said Yargi, staring at the book. 'They come to burn you... I won't let them.'

He rose and bit back the pain. For a careful moment he eased his weight back onto his bad leg. Pain lanced through and Yargi propped himself up against the wall clasping the journal — squeezing his pain into it. The steps summoned Yargi into the clear light and the owl beckoned him up each step with soothing hoots that promised everything would be alright.

Were the besiegers sleeping? What of the city folk? Alive? Dead? Curiosity found Yargi limping up the stair until it opened into the moon-bright night. No door, no ceiling, no jail. Just an almost-twelve-sweepscore-old stood shoulders above the ground where steps faded to rubble and ruin.

Fires burned about the crumbling city. Some were remnants of buildings shattered by flaming rocks. Some were merely cookfires tended by city folk huddled with their worries and warmth around blackened pots and struggling embers. Yargi clutched the book tight as he scanned the devastation. Most of the harbour ward had been crushed by trebuchet-tossed boulders.

Close by, beside the charcoal skeleton of a tree was an inert spider-shaped city breaker poised in attack. This one was constructed of stone components rather than iron. Whoever ended it must have ripped out the magia orb that usually glowed on its underbelly. The same glow that came from the wooden skeleton thing that had attacked him. The glow was nowhere to be seen... perhaps the rebels had taken it.

Magia had always been a precious commodity. Especially now Emlok had a monopoly on pretty much all of the magia mines. This mekanitek war engine now had a new job: shelter for a pitiful looking family. A dirty faced family clustered around a fire, children nuzzled up to mother and father like frightened piglets. From stone legs they had strung a line and on it dried filthy rags that

Yargi recognised as clothes.

'Boy! You there!'

Yargi cringed and turned.

'You, okay? You injured?'

A man, no one Yargi knew, was stood by a tripod from which a pot hung above a modest fire amidst the ruin of a half-demolished building. Yargi nodded then changed his mind and shook his head.

'What?' said the man, jerking a confused expression into his face. He wiggled his nose and rubbed the bushy moustache nestling beneath as he considered Yargi. 'Come on,' he said, gesturing with a nod to the pot, 'I have me some stew. It's nothin' much, but will plug a hole and heal light hurts.'

Yargi squeezed the life out of the book and did not move. The man laughed. His face falling to sympathy, eyes resting on the journal. 'I ain't gonna take your book. Gods know enough has been taken from us this last sunsweep. Now come on.'

There was something in the man's mild laughter that softened the fear in Yargi and it was Yargi's stomach calling out loud that settled the argument in his head. He put one foot ahead of the other and limped through the rubble until he was sat beside the man. The moustachioed man bore a lump on his head and soot on his cheeks. A grazed hand, rough and glinting fresh wounds in the firelight dutifully stirred the bulbous pot with misshapen ladle which Yargi imagined had either been found in a ruined kitchen, sat on or perhaps even used as a weapon.

The man gave no name, nor did he ask of Yargi's. He simply brought the stew to a simmer, cranking the pot up on its chain away from the flames and attended it with a pinch of this and that from a wax packet Yargi assumed contained herbs. When presented with a chipped bowl and a hunk of stale bread, he savoured the scent and warmth of cooked food.

Winter was creeping in. Yargi wondered, as the stew cooled, whether this would be the last warm food he would have for a while. He ate in silence. He ate as though it was his last meal.

'You eat as like a dead man breathing,' said the man.

Yargi raised an eyebrow.

'You know... like a prisoner who knows he'll be dangling the next day.'

Yargi made no reply and the man sniffed and continued his meal in silence. The man's words brought Yargi to remembering the last batch of executions. The ones that broke the city's obedience and ultimately brought Emlok's wrath upon Taz. Had citizens hiding in the ruins of their lives eating stew that was most likely rat based. There had been a Salfirin amongst them. *Could they have been...* Yargi's fingers found the journal and the urge to skip to the end settled heavy like the stale bread in his stomach.

He could not. Would not. Instead, Yargi finished the maybe-rat stew and in the flickering light, continued reading.

*I happened upon this aged letter in the forgotten libraries of Baajar where the once glorious city of fable and legend has all but been reclaimed by the jungle. The people here, mostly humans, have reverted to a simpler life since the Cataclysm. Yet, that does not imply they are not proud of their heritage and history or have fallen to barbaric tendencies. They dwell amidst the ruins of the Old World and have returned to the ways of Seodan and Exe. They worship the Son of Soil and have a huge head of Exe central in their round fort. My guide, Jarax, had promised a warm welcome and Baajarians did not disappoint.*

*It was over a few moonsweeps I managed to acquire an ear for their tongue and written word. Baajarian is not dissimilar to the more common Seodanish spoken by most humans. As a Salfirin scholar, I am fluent in all of Seodan's languages. Baajarian was simple, yet elegant. The most curious aspect of the Baajarians is their history and worship. We Salfirins are taught in Tanbenar that they were multifaith, both appreciating and dedicating themselves to the whole pantheon. I broached this topic with the chief who confirmed such had been the truth once. Yet, not now. Not since the Cataclysm. I am told, and with much pride, Baajarian soothsayers had predicted the Cataclysm. Their priests and priestesses claimed it was Exe's reprisal for the sullying of his shrine after the final conquest.*

*Now, Exe's head graces the centre of what remains of their once mighty civilisation. The Great Temple of long ago lies in ruin. Plundered after the last war. Of all the texts that survive, this letter proved fascinating to me and at the same time a warning for the times we live in. When another supposed great ruler stands to change the world forever. Particularly because this letter seemed to have gone undelivered. Why? What transpired to forestall its sending?*

# IN BAAJAR WHERE GODS STAND TOGETHER

My dearest Lindethi,

Find penned here, my final adventure in the Southern Lands. There is so much to tell you now. Yet these will be the last words of mine you read. I want you here, in Baajar. Come, in your caravan with entourage as soon as you read the last words inscribed.

In Baajar my dear, the southern city, stands a temple. Built of the finest dressed ashlar stone. Stone worked and heaved by enslaved hands. The pyramid rises flagrantly from paved ground where intricate carvings, long smoothed by pilgrims' feet, whisper ghostly incantations to the sky.

    This shrine. A battleground to myriad ancient gods and goddesses vying for tribute like peacocks with polished stone skin and jewel-encrusted features.

With a sack slung over my shoulder, to the temple I stride, reaching the first of five hundred and seventy-one steps. One for each day taken for our world to circle Sigik. Each footfall payment to the gods. Come the final step the entrance yawns where just within, this weary pilgrim is greeted by a goddess.

Salaria the saviour. The Redeemer. Mother of Deliverance. Radiant in flowing grey-veined white marble chiton. Tumbling locks flowing loose as does a cool breeze after battle down here in the south. One hand outstretched where once a delicate beckoning finger invited patrons into her embrace. Polished eyes speak, "Come with me and feel at peace." The fingers are gone, crumbled or smashed. The other arm lies in rubble at sandaled feet. She saved no devotees this day.

Within, a narrow passage draws on. Oil lamps light my foot falls to a circular chamber ringed in silver plate polished to divine lustre. Already strips are gone. Plundered beneath a blind gaze. Isatur the Watcher. Knower and Seer of All. Of flawless ice-clear quartz he is hewn. Ringlet beard coils to bow knees. Back bent in testament to eons of watching the world turn. His emerald eyes plucked out. He failed to see the looters coming.

The unadorned passage winds up surrendering the next chamber. Beneath the helmed gaze of towering Gastian, the Protector, I pause to catch my breath. The granite Guardian stretches ten men high to open ceiling above. Broadsword clasped in hands as expansive as mountains. Feet spread unremitting and unyielding, the blade between. To leave the chamber one must either retreat or pass a blade polished by the praying hands of devotees. I pass through but do not beg for his protection.

Sparsely lit, the way winds up more steps cut for gods through an opening, forcing a genuflection to Atika, Goddess of Oceans. You would find her a beauty to behold, my dear. Along stepping stones, I hop, for the chamber shimmers with a shallow salty pool in the high light of guttering oil lamps. Known as the Cleanser, the naked daughter of Seodan is resplendent in smooth turquoise curves rising from the clear pool. I stoop to wash the blood from my estoc blade and hands beneath her purifying smile.

A steeper climb follows. Tight and narrow. Before me then is the crumbling sandstone form of Exe, Son of the Soil. The most neglected of the gods. From fallen head, his solemn eyes stare into mine as I ponder who toppled this once mighty god.

The mail beneath my torn jupon weighs heavy with each step taken, yet further I go, coming upon Father Seodan & Mother Altilios. After the god and goddess, we named our world and moon. Did you know that? Father Seodan, carved of dappled bluish-green azurite and his lover, his equal in vibrant metallic gleaming labradorite. Moon to her companion's world. Offerings of food rotting and shattered vessels where patrons once donated jewels lie strewn beneath their rueful eyes.

Through a crawlspace no taller than a man's knees, I skulk, sending crested helm, sword and sack ahead to finally behold the vacant dais where once the solid gold goddess of fortune, Monetia, once reclined. I rest to puzzle the guile of the looter's skills, suspecting magia to have been involved in the emancipation of the voluptuous golden woman.

A breeze blesses my face and reminds me of your gentle touch. I restore my helm and secure my blade and I heave the sack up for the last time. The sky is closer and my journey almost complete.

Now in a spherical chamber, then down single-track steps to a stone hewn column upon which stands the Almighty, creator and bringer of life. Androgynous Sigik, colossal, muscular arms holding aloft Seodan and Altilios depicted as babes. I pay no mind and do not linger, knowing my goal is near.

The penultimate chamber and the focus of my

efforts arrives. I kneel before the purple obsidian statue of Conus, Goddess of War. Bringer of Doom. Merchant of Death. Our goddess, the one true goddess. The rites tumble from my lips as easy as the sack I carry leaves my sore shoulder. The gifts to our goddess roll out.

I slice my palm on the sharp sculpted blade Conus forever bears over a cupped obsidian palm patiently awaiting blood. I have brought further tributes this day. The heads of those who once ruled Baajar. I place them at her feet. My lips walk with invocations of victorious future battles.

I pass onward to the final chamber where dwells Imia, Goddess of the Underworld. Taker of the Dead. Mother of Corpses. Here I linger not. The onyx death goddess will not see my soul today. I have evaded her mongers of the soul. The narrow passage I take up scrapes my pauldrons, the low ceiling scratching my crested helm. So steep is the spiral vice ascent that I am breathless upon reaching the temple apex. Yet it is your image encouraging me onwards.

I survey land conquered at my command. The palace sacked by words I spoke. The city kneels to me. Below, on the temple steps, stretch the corpses of two looters I slew for stealing what is mine. At the base, the plump golden reclining figure of Monetia under heavy guard. I breathe deep of yet another victory as I stand with the gods.

Yet it is you, dearest Lindethi, whom I crave by my side. So come here, to Baajar and we shall stand upon the apex of the great temple together as Emperor and Empress in our rightful place.

Yargi yawned and rubbed the tiredness from his eyes. He continued reading defiantly, drifted, then woke with a start, caught the book in a fall and sat up. The fire had died and the man was curled beside it snoring. On the walls about the city, alert globes of fires hung, betraying soldiers in their watches. Down the hill where buildings slept at slanted and crooked angles, beyond and in the harbour, skeletal shapes of wrecked and broken ships glinted in the moonlight like corpses rising from the water. The harbour gates were shut, completing the seal of the city.

*It won't do any good*, Yargi reassured himself. The silent wooden soldier got in somehow. And the spider-like city breakers had been hurled amidst them. Sure, the city guard had dealt with them, but beyond those walls was the army of an empire.

He thumbed the written pages of the journal, resisting the urge to read the end before its time. Would he find out what happened to her, this Duyen? Yargi stared into the night sky. Not a forever dark. It would soon give way to day. And this quiet hush that had taken the city. Why *was* it so quiet? Emlok always made good on his promises. Everyone knew that. Yargi turned an ear to the closest wall, listening for the sounds of fighting beyond it. He heard nothing. No clunk-thunk-clunk, no click-clack-click. Nor the calls of Salfirin soldiers.

Wood and stone and iron... animated monsters, approximations of the many creatures of the world. Yargi had heard talk of such contraptions but never imagined anything as swift and alive as the thing in the old jail. Many rumours abounded in the empire though. It was hard to decide fact from fiction, but he assumed that was the point. Least, that was what poppa had told him. Yet to actually witness such a creation and have it pursue him...

'It's not safe here,' Yargi whispered to the book. 'We need to leave this place.' He looked around at the bunched-up masses, homeless and starving. They were broken, waiting for someone to win. Anyone. They would tolerate Emlok, so long as he fed them. *Not me.* Yargi told himself. He eased into a crouch and scanned the shattered buildings across rubble and ruin. *There has to be something.*

He crept away from the fire and found himself shocked at just how cold the nights were becoming. Prowling the crumbled building beside stray dogs and rats, he spent what felt like an eternity sifting through what was once people's lives. So loved, cherished; a doll his sister would have adored; a tatter of floral pinafore reminding him of his mother; a cap his poppa might have worn — this one had blood in it. Yargi dropped it immediately. All lost.

The first building of promise was a bakery gutted by fire. Perhaps an unchecked oven. It proved teeming with scrapping rats too fierce to bother with. A pack of dogs chased Yargi from the outfitters. He at least managed to make an escape with a new pair of trews and a jacket. Both dusty and slightly rubble-rough but better than what he already had on. A little way down the shattered terrace he found — after much digging — a leather satchel with a little bread wrapped in wax paper along with some hard cheese. He had to close his eyes when yanking the strap free from the hand protruding from the rubble. At least the bag would make its intended journey.

With the journal and meagre food and clothing tucked in the satchel, Yargi limped the shadows of the jagged buildings from street to nook to alley. Aside from a brief paranoid moment he thought he was being followed, Yargi came to the city wall. Sheer and solid, it stood between him and Ringwood beyond the city. Upon the battlements, guards patrolled and the odd fire punctuated their stations along it. They would stop him if he attempted to leave. He was just a boy after all. They would ask him where his parents were and it would come out that they—

Yargi looked back to the city and saw it whole again, in the daylight. Saw their smiling faces, his baby sister, just three sweepscores old.

—he would be sent to the orphanage. That was as good as the prison where he had discovered the book. 'We rest,' he told the book, patting the satchel. 'We rest. And when my leg is better, tomorrow at dawn's first light...' There was sure to be trouble. The guards would be occupied and he would find a way down the other side of the wall and steal into the forest amidst the commotion. No one would notice, nor care. Not about some child — not if he kept low.

Yargi eyed the shadows at the foot of the wall and spied what he was looking for. A kennel. With great caution — the dogs that guarded the wall were vicious, not to mention the noise one could make — he approached the battered kennel and noted the snapped tether. The kennel was empty.

It was cramped inside but no one would think to look in there. Not now. It reeked of its previous owner but that was fine. It felt good to have four walls and a roof. Yargi felt like a giant hiding from a mob of villagers in a tiny barn. He wedged himself up inside and tried to sleep, but it was no good. He was suddenly wide awake when he heard footsteps approaching and a pair of boots came to a halt right outside the kennel. He made himself so small and held his breath. The boots shuffled about as if the owner were searching for something or someone. Then, just when Yargi thought he could no longer hold his breath, they left.

Yargi sucked in air as his heart hammered. How would he rest now with his entire body poised to flee? Reading usually sent him off — a trick mother had taught him. Though, Yargi always suspected she had simply been training him to entertain his little sister, saving her a job. Yet there was something about reading that would take him away and seemed to make the world better. As if magia existed in the inscribed words. He unbuckled the satchel and hefted the journal into his lap and flicked to where he had left off.

*Seodan and the six races lay claim to some exquisite legends. Most have been told over crackling fires to young and old. I heard this story when I came to Gat, just north of Ham. I would later hear the same tale in a different tongue when in Rhodethå. Both tales bear their similarities and both were simply orally preserved until now. This is the only written form of a tale I believe to be a children's fable, or at least a cautionary anecdote.*

# OLDEST TRICK IN THE BOOK

'Some say it holds spells what give those who utter them dominion over all things. Guarded by a thousand dark souls. So some say,' said Blackeye, slurping ale wiping his brushy black moustache with a sleeve.

'I heard t'was magia so dark, so treacherous, s'why it's locked in a tower all the ways out there. Storms borne of that very same malevolent magia ravage the place,' rumbled Toeless, puffing pipe smoke like a fire mountain.

'Well, word in my ears was it bestows unto its master the gift of immortality. I've it in good confidence that wicked creatures dwell in them cliffs, devouring all what dare come near,' wheezed Hook Nose.

'Gift of immortality? Curse more like,' moaned Bow Back, bent over his tankard. 'Who wants to live forever in this wretched world? Things ain't what they used to be.'

'It mattuths not, anyhow. Therth ain't no one around that can swipth it. Bow Back's right, it's cursethd,' lisped Cut Lip.

'Can't swipe what?' came a voice as bold as those heroic, fearless, laudable types of ancient legend from behind the muttering men who were warming themselves beside the roaring hearth.

'The book. In the tower. On the island,' said Blackeye.

'I wager I could.'

'That you're the finest in the Guild of G'dai, Morg, goes unopposed,' said Toeless, 'but there's not one of us in the Guild who can steal a cursed book. Though many have tried...'

'I'm unsurpassed. Naturally I can steal a mere book.'

'If someone were to accomplish such a thing, they'd surely warrant the title of Greatest G'dai,' glided a voice so soothing, so sultry, a colossal granite-born berganor would quiver at the knees and crumble to nothing but shale.

'Ah, Starla, as exquisite as you are cunning. Yet not near as cunning as I. Oh how would it be to rest that fine backside of yours here enjoying these silky cushions of success?'

'Whatever Morg,' said Starla, rolling the remark

away with her eyes as she sauntered up behind the seated Morg. 'You're top dog. There's no question. Except...' She leaned on the high back of Morg's oak chair. A throne carved with legendry exploits of the guild of thieves and bandits.

'Except what?'

'Well, surely the question is obvious. Why *haven't* you acquired it?'

'That *is* a good question,' said Morg, crossing and uncrossing his legs. How could he be the best of all if he had not stolen this book? Immortality, 'ey? A tome like that could fetch a good deal of riches. 'I shall do it,' he thumped the arm of the chair, resolute. 'On the morrow, at first light.'

The hearth smouldered with remnants of the previous night's fire. Morg rose from claggy sweat drenched furs and stretched the ale aches from cold bones. The others snored. Strewn like hounds about the place under hide, fur and sheepskin. Morg's heart suddenly leapt. He stooped, tossing up sheepskins and furs in a livid frenzy.

'Starla? Starla! Where is she?'

'Heard her leave in the wee hours,' yawned Toeless.

Morg made him yelp with a boot.

'Why didn't you wake me? Fool!' He narrowed his eyes. *Starla. That crafty bird has flown for the isle, no doubt.* 'I won't be out done,' Morg yelled as he flung on his furs.

Morg slipped like a wraith from Guild Keep, through the strangling morning mists clinging to the Ulvern Mountains on his swift black palfrey, down twisting track and along stony trail. When the sun was halfway on its journey across the azure sky, he made the coast.

Two thumbs of silver bought a swift shallow draught ship to the hardy Isle of Rhodethå where even the fairest folk drank fermented fish liquor so strong it could drop a bereox with but a sniff. From the drunken Stoum port of Preta and across the legendary Bridge City of Nus, Morg worked his palfrey hard paying no heed to the night creatures stalking the wilds.

'I will not be out done,' he growled, teeth gritted against the frigid air as he galloped north.

From the desolate village of Ont, Morg cajoled an unenthusiastic fisherman into bearing him to the Isle of Wodha where the monks in residence were known to cut out their own tongues and wear sandals lined with tacks.

Onward north, into the icy winter flush to Knårda, a mountainous island growing defiantly from the sea. Already snow and ice had laid the land cruel and desolate. Exchanging boat for a sled pulled by trained vuveks, Morg sat wrapped in furs, beard frosted and glaciers growing in his eyes.

'I will not be out done,' he spoke frozen words through dancing teeth.

East now, and to the coast once more where Stoum live a severe life on the ice shelf bridging the sea to the islets where Starla no doubt had flown. Ahead, the twin islets rose like fingers of a drowning man, and upon the smallest stood the tower. The sled came to a halt.

'Why have you stopped?'

'The vuvek will go no further,' said the driver. She cast an anxious nod to the isles, 'nobody goes too close. Not there.'

'You would have me walk?'

She nodded, ruddy nose and cheeks glowing from within close drawn furs. She would have no silver, nor gold from him and when he threatened, her vuveks were quick to call. Teeth were swifter and more brutal than his dirk. Morg resigned to walking.

He left behind him the howl of vuveks and crack of the whip, turning into the snow-streaked sky and pressed on peeking through wrapped cloth and furs.

*This is no magia storm. No malevolent tempest.*

Morg grinned at foolish tales; no beasts lay in wait; nothing pounced when he placed gloved fingers in cracks and crevices as he clambered the rugged cliff to the foot of the crumbling tower. He stooped in the open entrance, a gaping mouth swallowing him into shelter.

*Not even a door?*

He laughed through stammering lips and warmed his hands with breath, rubbing life back into fingers. He would need them supple and deft. Morg shucked his furs to be light and fleet footed. Spiralling the steps upward, his feet seemed to make no sound, his clothes did not rustle and he appeared to have no need to breathe. The way was dark until Morg spied a flickering light and felt the subtle warmth of candle flame drifting through a low arch.

There in the circular chamber on a stone carved dais was the book. Leather bound and seemingly worthless and there, staring down on it in grim glare, a hooded man was painted and framed in gold.

*Perhaps I will take the painting too or perhaps just the frame, for melting down.* 'So, you are the final guardian?' said Morg to the painted man behind whom were rendered hooded folk, shifty eyed and crooked. Morg knew his own when he saw them.

*Painted thieves to guard a magia book?*

He laughed. Rumours. The only thing guarding this tome were rumours and the fools that feared such superstitious talk. Morg reached out to take it. For an instant his heart clenched, yet when his fingers brushed its cover, all was well.

He hefted the book.

It had a good weight and smelt of dry leaves. The painted thief's glare grew stronger or so it seemed. Morg considered the book. Immortality? Power beyond belief?

'Ah what the hell,' he said aloud and placed the book back on the dais prying open the stiff cover.

Searing pain cut through him. He could not scream. His breath left him as his bones flattened and skin became oil. The chamber span and the candle on the sill guttered out.

After a moment, a light blossomed in the dark illuminating the hand which conjured it. The hand bore the flame through the dark finding wick and wax. The room flowered into light once more, revealing Starla grinning broad and smug. 'Gotchya,' she said with a wink, and before leaving she cast a glance over her shoulder, patted her backside and blew Morg a kiss.

Morg wanted to scream, yet paint spoke words of pictures not sound. There he stood, immortal in oils, glaring as the most cunning of the Guild of G'dai sauntered beneath the arch taking the candle, stealing the light.

\* \* \*

*I traced Morg's path backwards, starting for those fingers and the tower of the fable. Indeed, there was a structure, and my Stoum guide was as equally reluctant to take me there, in keeping with the tale. Though gold was enough to turn his superstitions to enthusiasm. The tale neglected to mention the steps climbing that finger of rock from where we landed the boat on a stretch of jagged rocks.*

*I wonder if Morg had been too pig-headed to have noticed. If he was real of course. We did, and I left to ascend on my own. I discovered the tower. Though, the roof had long gone and part of the seaward wall too. If there had been a painting, it had most likely been whipped away by the tempests that often harry the islet.*

If this painting and book are real, Yargi promised himself, *I will find them*. He would find them and gift them to Emlok, somehow. Then he would burn both book and painting. There would be no coming back from that, would there? End of an empire, just like that. *You have to escape the city first,* his own mind told him. Yargi looked for the rising dawn yet still it was night. It had felt like an age in that world of ink and pages. He yawned.

The last few days were catching up on him. He rubbed his eyes trying to remember the last time he had properly slept. Yargi tucked the book away in his satchel and, like the dog that had once called the kennel home, curled down to get some sleep.

He dreamt viscous dreams. Was back underground in that cell, crushed beneath that rubble. Scratching, something was scratching. Something was under the rubble with him. Scratching... his leg! Claws clenched. He tried to scream. It was stifled as though there were no air in which for it to form. *Wake up*. The rubble tumbled revealing that wicked magia glow. *Wake up*. The silent soldier was there, clawing up him, dragging itself along him like some flesh ladder. Wake—

'—up!'

Yargi's scream broke the morning. He heaved

in a breath. Shot up awake. Banged his head and yelled again. The glow, not the dawn, but eyes of magia. Right there, breaching a hill of soil like some perverse mole and behind it, another iron skull. Right in the kennel's view.

*They dug... they're here.*

Yargi delayed no longer. He scrambled out of the kennel on all fours and scattered to the nearest steps intent on shouting alarm, but as his lips parted and a yell formed in his throat, others called out. Across the city, cries went up and there, from the first step, Yargi saw mounds popping up all over. They erupted from soil. From rubble piles. Poured from buildings they had surfaced within, scattering citizens from like rats evading a house cat.

*They had been digging all that time.*

Screams. Shouts. Cries for mercy.

Yargi turned to ascend the wall only to be knocked back by guards pouring down the steps. He hit hard, the wind left him and the bag spun from his clutch. Tramping feet filled his head. The clash of iron on iron. Yells of pain. *The book!* Yargi sat back up and looked about to where his bag had gone, head thumping.

*There*, 'No!'

A silent soldier was emerging from its crater,

the bag too close to the edge. Dread took Yargi and it was all he could do not to flee that moment. The book... they would burn it for sure. All those stories — lost.

'No!'

Yargi screamed and flung himself forward despite all reason. He snatched his satchel. The iron soldier grabbed him. He shrieked. The iron soldier's other arm cranked back to strike. Those eyes glowed vivid destruction. *I'm going to di—*

A crash. A crushing weight. The weight suddenly gone. 'What in the hells kid?' A city guard stood heaving with effort after pulling the silent soldier off Yargi.

'Th–thank–you. I'm sorry I—'

A blur. The guard suddenly gone.

Before Yargi could truly process what had happened, he was up and running for the steps again. A quick glance behind and he saw and heard the guard's crunching death. The silent soldier that had taken him down whipped its glare to Yargi.

He swept his bag strap over his head. He would not lose it. Not again. He flung himself toward the steps using his hands when he had to. The exposed stair zig-zagged up the curtain wall. A downward glance. The iron skeleton was after him. His lungs seared, his muscles felt as though they would tear and his feet and fingers burned with imminent blisters.

Zig after zag, Yargi pounced up the steps to find the battlements abandoned and — even though he knew it to be foolish — he looked out over the city. Wooden soldiers slunk in the shadows surprising guards and citizens alike. Iron soldiers fought one against clusters of guards. Stone soldiers, swept their granite limbs bludgeoning any fool who ventured too close. Others chased down citizens and units of them were already herding groups of citizens. City breakers clambered the ruins, driving survivors like a dog drives sheep into a fold.

A sound drew Yargi's attention to where he climbed up. The head of the silent iron soldier rose as if out of some dark mire. Yargi's stomach clenched and he backed away into a run. He turned fully, tracing the merlons along the battlement, trying to snatch a view through the crenels. Trying to make sense of the snatches of the world beyond.

Trees — the forest. He was on the right side at least. The one closest to Ringwood. Behind, the silent soldier strode after him. *Rope. Rope. Rope.* He prayed for it. It never materialised. 'No, it's not fair,' Yargi shouted as he lunged for the next stairwell and dropped down. The soldier was not far behind so Yargi allowed himself to half tumble the first flight to land on his knees. He cried out in pain, scrabbled to his feet and skip-jumped the next zag and leapt the last few feet to hit the ground in a roll which would have been well executed had he not twisted his ankle.

Hands and knees again, he fumbled towards the only exit he could think of; one of the molehills the silent soldiers had made. A thump behind told of his pursuer. Yargi crawled. He dragged. His body seared with effort. He was suddenly in the hole, tumbling through dirt and stone. He kept going and going and going. He would not look back.

Yargi surfaced after what seemed like a long worming crawl. Thoroughly muddy and exhausted, he heaved himself up and out into the day. Too weary to even check around or behind. He teetered into the trees and a bush hidden divot. He collapsed.

It was night when Yargi woke again. This city glowed with the magia aura of Emlok's forces and the battlements now dressed with his banners and flags bearing the sigil of his empire and the GLAS army. From his pitiful bush, Yargi watched, unable to cry. He sat there until the night faded to dawn, watching legions of magiatek war machines filing in and out of the city. Wagons crammed with what Yargi surmised to be prisoners of war.

He was weak. His body seemed broken beyond measure, but when he checked beneath his ragged clothes Yargi saw only heavy purple bruises and grazes that would leave his dark skin blotchy pink. His ankle throbbed, yet the goddess of luck had been smiling upon him. It was not broken. A small price to pay for his freedom. 'Told you I'd get you out,' he said to the book as he removed it from his satchel to check it was still there. Yargi made himself comfy in his hideout. It would be wise to rest a little. Besides, there was only a little left to read.

*The Tanbenantian Steppe is home to myriad tribes. Herders mostly. Robust peoples who earn their lives rearing zebuaco on the planes. The steppe freezes in winter and the berganor were said to bring the frosts. I remained with the few tribes who adhere to the old ways and customs and, though diverse in their traditions and attire, one unifying aspect is this legend below. I say legend, yet many of the witchdoctors and chieftains maintain them to be more than simple folkloric morals. Most believe it history.*

*I worry for the fragility of these people in these current political times. Emlok's armies are forging deeper into the Scorches now. Hunting down tribes like these and either assimilating them into his vision of the New World or destroying them along with any evidence of their culture. Emlok preaches homogeneity. All should be the same. The same beliefs. The same stories. The same behaviours. He judges lore such as that belonging to the people of the steppe as danger-*

*ous ideals and incitation to rebellion. I view them as the organic, natural lore of the world he fears and wishes to expel.*

*This legend, or history, is an amalgamation of the versions I heard whilst dwelling with these truly fascinating and invaluable peoples. It is rich in their culture and a call to action. Precisely the kind of writings Emlok fears.*

# TEARBLADE

'They're on the move,' said the old woman, wrangling her two-legged slori to rest. It beat its chest and settled with the peculiar whiny they made — somewhere between horse and ape — returning to its forelimbs.

'I've never seen so many,' said the young woman in furs beside her, upon her own stunt-legged slori mount.

The young woman had always found the pinch-faced monkey beast funny to look at. Ugly and insanely put together — the creation of some child god, perhaps. Yet, on the steppe, they served better than horses, especially in the craggy foothills.

Both old and young surveyed the snowy plane as giants of rock and ice languidly carved glacial valleys with their dragging feet. 'They take pleasure in this cold,' croaked the old woman, 'this winter has been the unkindest. The berganor,' she nodded to the ice giants, 'they come with creeping ice and sweeping snow.'

'Shaman Ifron claims winter is sent ahead of them. That they are Isbrid's children,' said the young woman, her slori rearing up at the mere mention of the spirit's name as if its simple mind understood. She calmed it with soft whispers then said, 'Do we see more berganor because of colder winters or are winters colder because of them? That's what the elders ask.'

'The elders have grown more foolish with each winter,' said the old woman as she breathed warmth into her bony fingers. 'They know the legend. They just choose to ignore it.'

'Tell me again,' said the young woman, as she watched the mighty ice giants carving up the steppe, 'tell me of Tearblade.'

'Again? Haven't you heard the legend enough?'

'Please. I need to hear it just one more time. From you.'

'Very well...'

Where the steppe was, the herd was. Fine, strong creatures. A sea of striped hide and twisting horn. Our people enjoyed a bountiful life. Meat and hide and fortune that comes with such things.

Where the steppe was, our people were. Tents, bold in colour, sturdy against the northern winds.

Our people were many, our influence felt far and wide. Music, food and tales and the fortune that came from such things.

But the summers came dryer and the grazing zebuaco grew in number as did we. More than the land could bear. The shaman warned the elders of the great clans that Isbrid, Spirit of the Land, had become angered. They heeded not her words.

Where the steppe was, was a winter fierce. So fierce, zebuaco froze where they grazed, herders iced over still mounted upon their slori and people became statues in their tents. Then came berganor with blizzards in their breath and cloaks of ice trailing their shoulders.

Where the steppe was, were the dead. The young, the old, the sick. Merciless winter stole many until few remained. Then came forth Sirabel. Thirty-five winters she had seen pass. Five children she had borne into the world. Five children she had lost to the ever-ferocious blizzards.

Wrapped in fur and hide, she rode her slori mount with a mind to beg Isbrid to cease this slaughter. Sirabel rode blizzards beneath the berganor. She rode beyond the frozen tents and herders and zebuaco. She called her slori to climb the foothills into the mountains trailing the great tongue of a glacier.

At the root of that glacier, Sirabel came upon

Isbrid, the spirit of the land. She cursed Sirabel for daring to come to her. Isbrid spat threats of ice and frost so sharp they sliced at Sirabel and she felt foolish for having come so far without a weapon. How could she, a herder, possess one though?

In despair Sirabel remembered those frozen to death on the steppe, the families, the herders, her children. Our people had spread too far and invoked Isbrid's implacable anger. Sirabel began to weep. She wept and wept and wept until, when she opened her eyes, she beheld a blade of frozen tears.

With nothing else she could do, Sirabel wielded the blade of tears to battle Isbrid and cut off the spirit's head and immediately the blizzard ceased. She rode to her clan triumphant, but with a warning; the surviving clans should not spread too far with their families and herds or Isbrid would return.

After suffering terrible losses and upon beholding the frozen blade along with the head of Isbrid, no one doubted her. The clans knelt before Sirabel and named her Tearblade. For a time, the blade of tears and Isbrid's head rested in a tent of their own. The winters grew mild and in time, both head and blade melted along with the snows.

Sirabel Tearblade governed the clans and bore more children from her loins vowing each girl she brought into the world, be it through her or through her progenies, would bear her name and with it the responsibility of retelling the time the clans were almost extinguished by an enraged spirit.

'Thank you. You tell it so well,' said the young woman, securing her furs tight against the howling wind.

'It is my duty as much as it is yours,' said the old woman, eyes creasing to a smile. 'As it was our name's sake, granddaughter.'

'Our herds have grown large once again. So too have our clans.' The young woman brought her slori about so they faced each other.

'And so too the ignorance of those in power,' said the old woman, tears freezing in her eyes. She kissed the young woman on the cheek. 'Go gently Sirabel. Our destiny awaits you.'

**D**estiny. Was it his destiny to find the book? To have escaped the city? Was he the only one who had? Yargi peaked down at Taz from the edge of the forest. GLAS guards were stationed now and the place seemed quieter and organised again. It was the last place he wanted to be. He shifted to stare into the forest.

Thick twisted growth glared right back at him. Testimony to forest once cleared and eventually abandoned to return in vengeance. A fortification of needle leaf and a prickly creeping tangle of thorn vine. Barrier against the West. A lot of good it had done. Emlok was patient and his GLAS army, tireless and persistent. They had cut through, widening the road. At least that was what folk had claimed, he had not seen it for himself. One thing he knew for sure: mekanitek did not require sleep, water or food. The fall of Taz was always going to happen. Yargi stood on wobbly legs, secured his satchel and stepped into the dark tangled wilds of Ringwood.

Deep night found Yargi with his back against a low crag in the forest. He would climb it tomorrow. Not today. When he had been confronted with the barrier his heart almost broke and that had been enough to tell him it was time to rest. Time to rest and warm himself with a modest fire and occupy his thoughts with a little more reading. Anything to quell the rising paranoia within him.

Yargi had expected the deep forest to be a quiet, tranquil place. The fringes had always seemed so compared to the thrum of the city. It was nothing of the sort. A tree crowded den of noise was what it was. Hoots and toots and shrieks. Snaps of twigs and creaks. Old wood moaning in the wind as their own leafy canopies hushed them. The feeling of many eyes watching. Of followers hidden in the murk.

Pushing aside the notion of stalkers in the low light, Yargi focused on the journal and those final inked pages.

*So here I find myself. In the walled city of Taz and caught up with Emlok's presence. The city is in his control and that control is fear, yet there is something lingering in Taz's citizens... they are not at ease. It is only a matter of time before they revolt. I can sense it. It is clear in their eyes and in their whispers of malcontent. Something will break their reluctance to take action. Some catalyst. Of that, I am certain.*

Yargi turned the page...

*Betrayed. The folk I was lodging with were GLAS sympathisers. I shared too much of my love for the writings of the world Emlok is attempting to wipe away. The authorities took everything away from me. My notes, my other books and collections I gathered. Everything except this journal which I had taken to strapping to my lower back with bandages after entering this broken city. I made claims of an infectious disease when the jailor pried. Thankfully, a doltish man, he bought the lie.*

*As I was dragged to my prison, I glimpsed faces in the crowds that had gathered to watch the spectacle of my so-called capture. Shocked to see Salfirin arresting their own, perhaps. At least some now know my kind are not all bent on subjecting the other races to their whims.*

Yargi swallowed an *oh no* and flicked to the next page so hastily, he almost tore it...

*I am to swing by the neck until dead. In the city square. This coming dawn. And in some obscene sense of relief, I am not miserable. I will not witness the utter end of this world's histories. Its poetry and prose... its myriad cultures. I still hope that after my death, someone will be courageous enough to carry the spark of this world's richness. To be a custodian of cultures as I sought to be. To kindle that ember and set it blazing once again. That is why I now hide this journal in darkness for it to someday see the light again.*

The last pages Yargi thumbed were definitely blank. Though he had hoped for something more, some mark, some word or illustration. There was nothing and there was a moment he felt a deep sadness about that. As if losing an old friend. Yet, she was still there, wasn't she? The Salfirin woman he had never met but felt like he had. Every letter, every word... there were still the parts written in Salfirin to translate.

Yargi vowed to learn the language, somehow. He would translate more stories. He would release more tales into the world. He flicked to the map at the front of the journal and stared at it for a lost while. Each hinted cove and bite of a bay, each nobble of land and expanse of continent and that dashed line, her footprints in paper grains. There was still so much left to explore. So many paths to be discovered and trails yet to be inked. So many stories, just waiting to be heard. Countless stories. All waiting to be captured in his own hand. But first it would all start with something so very simple. It would start with a crag, he would—

A snapping twig. Yargi's thoughts cut dead.

Before he could smother the fire. Before he could gather his meagre belongings. Before he could hide. A figure came out of the gloomy tangle of forest and stepped into the modest fire light. A Salfirin soldier. The soldier's eyes fixed on Yargi, then the journal. 'You're a hard one to track.'

Yargi glanced the fire and glared at the soldier. Flames in her eyes. He clenched the journal tight. 'I won't let you burn it.'

'What?' said the soldier. She looked at herself and laughed. 'Oh, the uniform,' she laughed. 'I am no soldier, *believe* me. I have no love of Emlok's lies and deceit.'

'Why have you been following me?' asked Yargi, unconvinced that this was not some sort of GLAS tactic. Some scheme to trick him into lowering his guard.

The Salfirin crouched, levelling with him. The firelight seemed to soften her features a little now she was not up lit. She nodded to the journal. 'Because you have something of mine.'

Yargi squeezed the book. 'This? This is not yours.'

'Oh? How do you know that?'

'Because the person who wrote this... she is dead.'

The Salfirin seated herself in cautious measured movement and rested cross legged. She smiled. 'I can assure you I am very much alive. Despite efforts to have me hanged.'

*Hanged*? How did she know? Yargi narrowed his eyes and said, 'If this is yours, then tell me... what is written on its pages?'

The Salfirin's smile broadened. 'It seems my journal found somebody courageous enough to carry our world's richness after all.' She paused as if waiting for some recognition and when it did not come, she continued. 'When I returned to the cell for the book and found it gone, I imagined the worst.'

*She escaped? How?*

'You're wondering how I am here, aren't you?' said the Salfirin. 'The day before my execution, there was a revolt. I was forgotten in the chaos, the siege ensued. A great rock struck the place where I was imprisoned. It was then an easier task to pull free the loosened bars in the arch and escape. I left my journal. Fleeing hastily as I feared the roof might collapse. When I returned, the book was gone and... well, I take pleasure in telling stories, so, if you are willing to hear me out, I shall start from the very beginning.'

She introduced herself as Duyen Fian and said that was not so important. She said she was indeed Salfirin, which was. She said she was a chronicler which was not so vital to know, but indeed, was vital to her work and had led her to this fire right here, with him, young bastion of lore.

# ACKNOWLEDGEMENTS

My greatest thanks to my wife and her keen eye for little details. To Karlos, who read most of these stories the first time round. Your feedback really helped, cheers. And to all those of you who helped choose the cover... many thanks!

# ABOUT THE AUTHOR

## M. F. Alfrey

A writer, artist and Sci-Fi & Fantasy geek. His love for SF & F seriously affects his ability to function in the conventional plane of existence. Besides that, he runs long distances occasionally and has a more than healthy obsession with roleplay games. He lives in a fantasy world with his wife and their growing dice collection.

Discover more from this author at syntheticlifeforms.wordpress.com

Printed in Great Britain
by Amazon